Cruising along Nostalgia Lane

by

Cynthia Breeding

Cruising along Nostalgia Lane

Contact Information: info@thewildrosepress.com

Cover Art by *Lisa Dawn MacDonald*

The Wild Rose Press, Inc.
PO Box 708
Adams Basin, NY 14410-0708
Visit us at www.thewildrosepress.com

Publishing History
First Edition, 2023
Trade Paperback ISBN 978-1-5092-5258-9
Digital ISBN 978-1-5092-5259-6

Published in the United States of America

"I think I like this set the best of all of them."

Sam nodded. "It looks like they saved the best for last."

"And it's different," Jill said. "We've had Sixties-based themes all week."

"A pirate theme is fitting, though, given that Jean Lafitte operated in both New Orleans and Galveston," Dawn said. "And, he was probably the last of the famous pirates—"

"Privateers," Cindi corrected.

"Whatever. It's still fitting since this is our last lunch on board, too."

The antics on stage continued as they ate their lunch, which consisted of a spicy shrimp Creole with French baguettes and crème brûlée for dessert. Just as they were finishing, there was a shout from one of the actors on the stage.

"Stowaway! We've got a stowaway!"

Several of the "pirates" gathered on the foredeck, where the lid of the water barrel had been pried open and a man was being helped out. He was bearded, and a bandana covered his head. He wore only a vest, showing muscular, tanned arms, and tight, ragged shorts that showed off equally muscular legs.

Dawn grinned. "Kind of like a male version of the girl stepping out of a bachelor party cake."

"I didn't know we had any Chippendale-type guys on board," Sue said.

"Well, he may not be a Chippendale, but he'll do," Dawn looked at Sam. "I guess you were right. They did save the best for last."

"I…" Sam frowned. There was something familiar about the stowaway…

Prologue

May 1969

Trust Jack O'Neill to pull something off. At least it wasn't his pants, as he'd been threatening to moon the audience of proud parents, grandparents, and dignitaries at the graduation of the Class of 1969.

Samantha "Sam" Olson shook her head as she pushed a stray curl back under her graduation cap. She doubted the folks of Gainesbury, Texas, population 2,506, would ever have been the same if Jack had followed through with his antics. It was bad enough he'd managed to conceal several frogs under his gown as they marched into the school auditorium. She'd seen him release them as they passed by the speaker's podium. It was only a matter of minutes before Mrs. Jones, a local pastor's wife, would step forward to deliver the invocation, and she'd totally freak out.

Sam let her glance slip sideways as she took her seat on the makeshift bleachers on the stage. Jack was sitting in front and slightly to the right of her, looking angelic. Which, of course, was part of the problem. He *always* looked angelic, with his mop of burnished gold hair that fell over his forehead and eyes as azure blue as the Texas sky. Most of the girls thought he was a real hunk. Coupled with an easy smile that showed a dimple in his left cheek and perfect manners whenever he was questioned, he never got blamed for anything. And *that* list was long…

As if he sensed her watching him, he turned his head and gave her his disarming smile. Except that she was not disarmed by it. Having lived next door to him for ten years, she'd witnessed far too many of his pranks and even been the victim of some, much to her chagrin. Now she narrowed her eyes at him, silently letting him know she'd seen the frogs. That only made him widen his grin and give her a wink before facing the front again.

It was a good thing they wouldn't be attending the same college in the fall.

The school band began the "Star Spangled Banner" and everyone rose as the ROTC color guard presented the flag. Mrs. Jones stepped to the podium as the anthem ended and, only a second later, emitted a shriek that rivaled any soprano hitting the high F in the "land of the free" line. Papers that had been placed on the podium so speakers wouldn't have to carry them went flying everywhere as Mrs. Jones grabbed the stand in an attempt to levitate herself above the now-hopping frogs.

The audience sat in stunned silence as the class of 1969 tried not to titter, although a few laughed outright. Definitely not cool right now. The principal, Mr. Wilhelm—a man with the bearing of a general—glared at the class, in particular Jack, as he marched across the floor.

Jack wore a benign look as though he, too, was bewildered by the chaos.

Sam just hoped they would receive their diplomas this evening. Their principal, a direct descendent of German settlers who'd come to Texas in the 1800s, was not known for his sense of humor. She was pretty sure he didn't have one.

By this time, the pastor had gotten on the stage and was escorting his still nearly hysterical wife away. Father Hernandez, priest of the local parish, stepped forward to take her place, but he, too, paused to look at Jack. Sam recalled that the kindly priest had attempted to make Jack an altar boy at one time. His stint was short-lived, although she never found out why.

It took several more minutes to corral the frogs, and Sam glanced at Jack again, wondering if he had any other surprises for tonight. Once more, he caught her eye. She frowned at him, but he just smiled. An infuriatingly innocent-looking smile.

Thankfully, he had no further pranks planned—or maybe he actually wanted to receive his diploma—and the rest of the ceremony went smoothly.

Sam sighed in relief as their names were read and they proceeded across the stage. Perhaps the earlier chaos that Jack had created was somewhat symbolic of their past years. They'd witnessed several assassinations, along with anti-war protests and Civil Rights riots. Perhaps, like the second half of this evening, now things would begin to smooth out.

The band played the school's fight song and, as they filed out, the choir began to sing the 5th Dimension's "Age of Aquarius."

Soon it would be the beginning of a new decade and the Graduating Class of 1969 would face it with that in mind.

Chapter One

Early December 2019

Sam paused on the Harborside Drive quay at the Port of Galveston and looked up at the cruise ship docked alongside. Compared to other cruise lines, the Good Times ships were small, each serving only three hundred passengers. The private line also had only four vessels, each theme-based to a particular decade of the twentieth century. The one she was currently looking at was *Sixties A-Go-Go*, and it would be home to the Graduating Class of 1969 for the next week as they celebrated their fiftieth reunion.

"You don't look old enough to remember the Sixties."

Sam turned to see who had spoken. A well-dressed man with dark hair just beginning to turn silver at the sideburns smiled at her. She hoped he wasn't one of her graduating class since she didn't recognize him.

"Well, you know what they say. If you remember the Sixties, you weren't there."

The man laughed. "I suppose that's true. I wasn't exactly the Woodstock type."

She supposed he wasn't, since she had a hard time imagining him with long hair, tie-dyed T-shirt, and scruffy sandals. He looked more like a CEO.

She smiled. "I didn't get to Woodstock either. My

parents were pretty uptight."

"So were mine." He held out his hand. "The name is Bond." He grinned. "*John* Bond, not James."

She laughed at his dry sense of humor and shook his hand. "Sam Olson." When he lifted an eyebrow, she added, "My parents named me Samantha." She gave him an inquiring look back. "Are you taking the Sixties cruise?"

He nodded. "Actually, I'm the editor for *New Escapes* magazine. We cater to a clientele that prefers out-of-the-way places not packed with tourists. Cruise lines are big industry, of course, but our readers don't like the huge floating cities."

"This should fit the bill, then."

"I hope so," he answered. "Will you be on board as well?"

"Yes. My class is celebrating their fiftieth reunion, and we decided to spend a week at sea to do it."

"Fifty years." He paused. "It hardly seems possible, does it?"

Where had all that time gone? Sam asked the question after John had excused himself to take a call. Her classmates had scattered all over the country after graduation. They'd held a reunion at the tenth year that was largely not remembered since a lot of them had been stoned or otherwise inebriated. By the twenty-fifth reunion, they'd rejected the theme of not trusting anyone over thirty, since they'd already surpassed that age and most of them had turned into the squares they'd thought their parents had been.

Somehow, another quarter of a century had slipped by.

Sam was looking forward to seeing the other seven

members of the Cicadas, the all-girl band they'd formed in high school. For a moment, her mind flitted back in time. After the second British invasion in the mid Sixties, garage bands had popped up everywhere, the guys all wearing their hair in mop-tops or trying to appear super cool like the most popular "invaders." A couple of her friends—Laura and Sue—had fantastic voices and regularly sang solos with the school choir, but none of the hip bands would let them join. Finally, out of defiance—and perhaps a precursor to Women's Lib— they'd decided to form their *own* band and recruited Jill, Cindi, Dawn, and Lynda to play drums, guitars and piano. She'd managed the band and another friend, Amy, had taken care of the props and equipment. As one of their heroes sang ten years later, they didn't need "no education," and the Cicadas had proudly announced in 1969 that they didn't need any guys on their team, either.

She'd hoped to run into some of her friends on the Strand or in Galveston's other gift shops earlier, but no one had looked familiar. Surely, she would recognize them? Her job with National Parks and Wildlife had kept her moving around and, although she'd stayed in touch as much as she could, technology often didn't work in the places she was sent to, or it was patchy at best. She hadn't actually seen any of them in years.

Hopefully, now that she'd retired she'd have more time and opportunity to renew those friendships. That was one of the reasons she'd suggested their class take a week-long cruise around the Gulf of Mexico. It would give them more time to reconnect.

As she walked up the gangplank to board, she wondered if Jack would be there. The card he'd returned to the committee had said he wasn't sure he'd be in the area. He'd missed the twenty-fifth, since he'd been in Australia commanding an oil tanker. His parents had moved out of her neighborhood before then, so she hadn't seen him since the tenth reunion, at which time he'd managed to scare nearly everyone who wasn't blitzed with a harmless kingsnake, claiming it to be a deadly coral.

She shook her head as she pulled out her passport and ticket for the officer waiting aboard. The ship's captain probably wouldn't appreciate snakes—or frogs—aboard any more than their principal had on the stage those many years ago.

****

Humming to the tune of "Galveston" playing over the loudspeaker, Sam saw three of her old friends immediately as she walked out on the lido deck at the stern of the ship later that afternoon—Dawn, who'd played bass guitar, Laura, who'd done lead guitar, and their drummer, Lynda. That the three of them would be huddled together already wasn't surprising. Even though the Cicadas had broken up after high school, this trio had stuck together. She waved as they looked up and saw her.

"You haven't aged a single year, I swear!" Laura, ever the dramatic one of the group, declared.

"I dare say she is quite right." Dawn, obviously still the lover of all things British, said in an affected accent.

Lynda nodded. "I'd recognize you anywhere. You look great."

She doubted that. Although her hair was still strawberry blonde and she hadn't gained weight, decades of working outdoors in all types of weather was hardly conducive to having a peaches-and-cream complexion. Even the best of moisturizing creams couldn't erase the sun lines etched around her eyes. Her friends were being kind… Or perhaps, judging from the empty glasses pushed to the middle of the table, they were working on their second and third margaritas and their vision was a bit blurred.

"Thanks," she replied as she sat down. "You guys look good too." It was pretty much the truth, considering they were all officially senior citizens. Laura's hair was still red, although perhaps enhanced with salon color, and she wore it shoulder-length like she always had. Dawn's hair was still blonde, too, although one of the blessings with light hair was that it didn't show gray as easily. Lynda had kept her sun-bleached tresses short, but given that she also sported permanently tanned skin, the streaks were probably natural. Truly, though, none of them looked their age. Or maybe she just didn't want to admit it.

As if by magic, a fresh margarita appeared in front of her by the hand of a waiter who whisked away the empties, adeptly holding several by their stems in each hand as he winked at the group.

Dawn giggled as he left. "He's good too. Quite well-trained."

Lynda rolled her eyes. "The more flirtatious he is, the better his tips."

"Don't be a downer," Dawn said. "This trip is kind of like that old TV show *Love Boat*. Who knows which of us will find a guy?"

"Forget me. I'm married," Laura said.

"Well, I'm not, and neither is Lynda or Sam."

"Leave me out of that picture." Lynda shook her head. "One marriage was enough, thank you."

Dawn turned to Sam. "What about you? Would you

like to meet someone?"

She wasn't about to mention John Bond. It had only been a one-minute casual conversation, after all. She wasn't a silly twenty-something to think he was *interested.* She smiled. "I suppose if some Viking warrior of old came striding across the deck, I might."

Laura laughed. "I'd forgotten how obsessed you used to be with history."

"Well, there's lot of evidence that the Vikings came to America long before Columbus did."

"Oh-oh," Dawn said. "Now we've got her started."

"I think we're on the wrong cruise if you expect to find a Viking here," Lynda said. "You may have to content yourself with Mayan ruins instead."

"Maybe an ancient god will pop up at one of them," Dawn quipped.

"If he does, I will welcome him into the twenty-first century," Sam replied with mock seriousness.

Lynda gave her a long look. "I think you probably would."

Sam took a sip of her margarita. It was true that she—and Cindi as well—were something of history buffs. She'd seen an old movie about Christopher Columbus when she was in grade school that had piqued her interest. By the time she'd gotten to middle school, she'd discovered that Leif Erickson—and more importantly, his father Erick-the-Red Thorvaldsson— had been to the "New World" before Columbus ever thought of taking a ship west. She'd been elated, since she was the descendent of Norwegians. Unfortunately, Jack had caught her acting out an imaginary scene in her backyard, brandishing a wooden sword and wearing horns from an old Halloween costume. She grimaced.

He'd relentlessly teased her, even calling her a Valkyrie, to which she'd retorted he'd better be careful because Valkyries decided who got to go to Valhalla.

"Why the frown?" Lynda asked. "Don't you like the margarita?"

"It's fine." She put the glass down. "I just recalled Jack O'Neill teasing me about my love of Vikings. Stupid how some memories linger."

"Well, he would be the one to do something like that," Laura said.

Dawn laughed. "He did seem to like teasing you. I think maybe he was sweet on you."

"Don't be ridiculous. I lived next door. I was an easy target."

"Um." Lynda raised a brow. "I wonder if he'll be on the cruise."

"I don't know. He was noncommittal on the RSVP."

"Typical." Laura paused. "I think my husband said he heard something about Jack having bought a sailboat and cruising the Caribbean."

"Then maybe, if he isn't on this ship, we'll meet him on the water!" Dawn grinned. "Like a pirate!"

"You always did have an overactive imagination," Lynda said. "Besides, we're sailing throughout the Gulf, not into the Caribbean."

Dawn waved a hand dismissively. "Whatever."

Whatever, indeed. Sam could almost see him bringing his boat alongside, demanding to be allowed on board, not that she was going to encourage Dawn's imagination. But…it would be just the kind of prank Jack O'Neill would do.

****

The rest of the group met up with them at dinner.

They'd chosen the late sitting in the formal dining room, which meant they could linger after their meal.

Sam looked around the large round table after they'd made their selections for appetizers. Cindi, their pianist, had hardly changed at all. She wore her chestnut hair in the same pageboy style she'd worn in high school and she had one of those pleasant faces that looked like she was perpetually smiling. Jill, who'd played flute and tambourine, had some streaks of gray in her dark hair and she sported rimless spectacles. Amy, their ever-patient props-and-equipment manager, had gone completely silver and short-cropped her hair. And Sue, their lead singer, was still striking, with curling ebony locks that contrasted with her ivory skin and blue eyes. Sam smiled inwardly. Their music might not have been sensational, but Sue had always managed to capture attention. She probably still did.

She lifted the glass of Cabernet the waiter had poured for her before he left. "To the Cicadas! Reunited once more."

"Although, hopefully, not to sing," Jill said as they all raised their glasses. "I think I'd feel silly banging my tambourine now."

Sue laughed. "I'll bet you wouldn't if you heard one of those songs we used to cover."

Jill rolled her eyes. "I can't believe how I thought pills were cool at the time."

"At least, you never tripped," Amy said.

"But I did come close once," Jill replied and looked at Cindi. "You were the one who convinced me not to."

Cindi shrugged, coloring a little. "I just never thought drugs were good."

"Hard convincing kids of that then," Amy said.

11

"It was probably a good thing we were all still in high school and our parents kept an eye on us," Cindi answered.

"Still. I wanted so bad to go to San Francisco for that Summer of Love." Jill shook her head. "I probably would have even worn some flowers in my hair."

"In retrospect, we were probably lucky we lived in a small town where everyone knew everyone else's business. We couldn't get away with much," Sue said. "Remember when Jack O'Neill got caught with pot?"

Sam almost laughed. It was one of the few time he'd ever gotten caught at anything. The ironic part was that he'd *found* the pouch on the street where some looped kid had probably dropped it without even noticing. No one else had believed Jack when he'd protested his innocence—talk about crying wolf one too many times—but she had. He had a habit of running his hand through his hair when he was actually serious about something, and he'd done it repeatedly while proclaiming his innocence. Still, she couldn't resist goading him a little first. While he might have annoyed her—*did* annoy her—the one thing she knew he valued was his ability to keep a sharp mind. Pulling pranks wouldn't be any fun—and very likely wouldn't be very successful—if he were stoned out of his gourd.

"His parents grounded him for a month," she said. "I remember seeing him at his window, glaring out at me."

"He's lucky he didn't get arrested," Cindi said.

Sam nodded. 'True." Their local police department had consisted of three officers. The one on duty that night had a son only a year older and, as he told Jack's father, he wouldn't want his own kid having a record for doing something stupid. "Another benefit of living in a small town."

"Yes," Jill said. "Lots of good memories."

Sam looked at the group as she had a sudden inspiration. "We do have good memories. Why don't we each share one that we're particularly fond of?"

"Tonight?" Sue asked. "I wouldn't know where to begin."

"No. It would take too long for everyone to share tonight." She thought a moment. "How about each one of us sharing one specific story each night after dinner? That way, we could prolong our trip along nostalgia lane."

"Good idea," Cindi said. "Why don't you start?"

"Um. Okay. Well, since we've been talking about Jack, there is one story that comes to mind." Sam curled up one corner of her mouth. "It was the night I almost murdered him."

****

Sam's story: 1965

I remember lightning flashing across the darkening sky as my sister and I crossed an open meadow. We'd been camping in the woods, and my dad always made me take a shotgun along, just in case we had to scare off a javelina or a coyote. The heavens opened just as we reached the shelter of some big trees.

"Wow! That was close," my sister Theodora—Teddi—said.

"Yeah," I answered as another fork of lightning streaked across the sky. "And trees aren't the best place to be in a storm." I remember looking at Teddi's wet clothing, too. "We'd better try to find some decent shelter."

Unfortunately, there was nothing close by. I thought I remembered an old cabin deeper into the woods, although I had an uneasy feeling about going farther in. Still, we didn't have much choice. It wasn't like I could beam us home via Scotty's transporter on the *Enterprise*.

Teddi spied the cabin a little later as we rounded some boulders near a stream. "Let's hope the door isn't locked!"

We climbed the three rickety steps to the porch. I remember them groaning and creaking and that I hoped a board wouldn't break. Teddi peered in through a window while I tried the door.

"Gosh, it's black inside," she said.

I heard the quiver in her voice and decided I needed to be the brave one. I was fourteen, after all, and she was just ten. "Don't worry. Just hurry up and get in. The storm is getting worse."

For a moment Teddi looked mulish and I thought she would dig in her heels, but then thunder crashed practically on top of us and she sprinted in.

Once inside, I turned on my flashlight and almost wished I hadn't. The thin gleam of light revealed two old, half-rotten benches nailed against a wall, a much gnawed-on table, and an old fireplace, although there was no dry firewood inside. The place smelled damp and musty, and from somewhere in the back a shutter banged shut.

Teddi turned big eyes on me. "Do you think it's haunted?"

"Haunted? Of course not!" I remember hoping I sounded convincing because I thought I heard something rustling in another room. To distract my sister, I said, "Let's see if these benches make good beds."

"You want to go to bed?" she asked. "Already? It's only…" She stopped as another heavy roll of thunder shook the glass in the windows.

"It'll be better if we go to sleep," I answered. "When we wake up, the storm will be over."

That seemed to pacify Teddi, and she settled in, but I remember lying awake, practically feeling my ears perk up for any sound. I had the feeling we were not alone, but I told myself I was letting my imagination run wild. I did lay the shotgun down beside me within easy reach, though.

It didn't take too long before I heard it. Another soft rustling. Then…footsteps? I remember thinking I'd been really stupid not to check out the place first. There was a hallway that led to the back area. Who knew what could be in here? A wild animal? Maybe some fugitive? Or even druggies that we'd awakened? Night had come early with the storm, and it was hard to see very far.

My hand clutched the shotgun as I rose to go over to Teddi. I shook her awake, putting my hand over her mouth to make sure she knew to be silent.

Something crashed loudly, followed by a grunt. I couldn't tell if it was a human sound or not. Teddi whimpered, although she didn't say anything. I raised the shotgun as I heard footsteps.

Then they stopped. I remember trying to see down the hallway, but it was too dark. Then the footsteps started again, still sounding only half-human but definitely much closer. Then I heard heavy breathing. You know what they say about your hair rising on your arms? It's true. I felt like at any minute I'd start crackling with static electricity. I steadied my hand on the trigger.

Lightning suddenly flooded the room, and I saw

Jack step out into the room. I swear I saw the whites of his eyes as he realized I had a gun trained on him, and he took a massive jump to the side, landing on the floor with a hard thump. In that instant—which really seemed like one of those slow-pause, time-stands-still moments in the movies—I thought maybe I'd pulled the trigger and killed him…

****

Sam shuddered and closed her eyes. Maybe this hadn't been the best memory to bring up.

"We know Jack is alive," Cindi said gently, "but *did* you shoot him?"

Sam opened her eyes and shook her head. "I pulled the trigger… I think it was instinctive, but by some Divine intervention, I swung the gun in the other direction."

Everyone was silent for a moment before Lynda spoke.

"So what was he doing there?"

"Good question." She was beginning to feel a little better. "He said he'd been out in the woods when the storm hit, and when he found the cabin, he didn't know we were in it."

Jill looked skeptical. "But you didn't believe him?"

"You think he followed you just to scare you?" Amy asked.

"I don't know. I couldn't get him to admit it, but I know he knew we were going camping."

"Well, if it was a prank, he should have learned his lesson," Dawn said.

"Should have, but didn't," Laura replied. "Remember graduation? And about a dozen other incidents?"

"He was incorrigible," Sue said. "I wonder if he still is?"

"Maybe we'll find out if he's here," Amy said. "The whole class is meeting in the morning."

"Meanwhile…" Sam took a deep breath. "I suggest whatever stories the rest of you decide to tell they will be a little less fraught with actual danger than mine."

At least, she hoped they were.

Chapter Two

Sam looked around the Oasis Lounge the next morning as the ship slowed its speed and prepared to anchor off the shore of Cancun, their first stop. The bar last night had been hopping, a disc jockey playing mostly beach-oriented tunes in anticipation of white sand and turquoise water today. This morning the bar was deserted, smelling slightly of stale beer, while "Surfer Girl" played over the PA system.

But they weren't here to drink at this hour. Her class had reserved the lounge for their initial meet-and-greet and to officially call the roll of those members present. A bulletin board had been brought in so they could sign up for on-board events with classmates as well as inland excursions. Even though the ship's capacity of three hundred was small, it would still be easy to miss each other otherwise. Although the girls of the band planned to mingle with the others, they'd probably be sticking together for the most part. Their husbands hadn't been able to attend for various reasons, which gave them a wonderful week for themselves.

She spotted her friends at a round table off to one side. Cindi and Laura looked rested since they hadn't been interested in the bar scene. Amy had joined them for a little while last night, but then drifted off too. Dawn was sipping tea, still attached to British customs, while Sue was nursing a coffee. Jill had her nose in the itinerary for the day.

Sam walked to the bar and helped herself to a cup of coffee while she scanned the room. It was still fairly empty and she saw no sign of Jack. She hadn't seen him last night either, but there were several bars on board. She gave herself a little shake as she went to join her friends. Why was she thinking of him after all these years?

"I don't think he's here," Jill said when she sat down.

Trust Jill to be the perceptive one. She had a degree in psychology, after all. Or maybe she'd seen Sam looking around the room. She'd never been a good poker player.

"Are you talking about Jack?" she asked anyway.

"Who else? After that story last night, I think we'd all like to see him again."

"Alive, of course," Lynda said dryly. "We could congratulate him on his narrow escape and maybe get him to confess that he intended to scare you."

She raised one brow. "I doubt it matters, fifty-some years later."

Lynda shrugged. "Still. The guy practically got away with murder himself, considering all the pranks he pulled in school."

The others all started laughing and recalling incidents. Sam laughed with them, having forgotten just how daring he'd been. Not only that, but most of the time when she got into trouble herself, it was because he'd put her up to something. It would be good to see him again and maybe turn the tables. She looked toward the door. The lounge was filling up now, the noise level increasing as more and more classmates recognized and greeted each other.

But by the time they were ready to walk down to the departure deck, he had not shown up. She felt an odd stirring of disappointment because she suspected—even if he was still a prankster—the cruise would have been a lot more fun with him.

****

The sun, reflecting off the white sand, was nearly blinding when they stepped off the canopied tender that had brought them to shore. The crystal-clear waters looked more like a vast swimming pool than the Caribbean Sea.

Sam scanned the water where a few sailboats were gliding gracefully along the horizon. Was one of them Jack's? She gave herself a shake for her fancifulness. The next thing she'd be doing was thinking of him striding across the deck of the *Sixties A-Go-Go* like the pirate Dawn had described. Or maybe he'd rise up out of the sea like Neptune…or whatever name the Mayans had called the sea god. Good grief! She hadn't expected such nostalgia over a reunion, even if it was their fiftieth.

"This sure beats the muddy coast of Texas," Lynda said as she adjusted her straw hat and put on sunglasses. "I may be spoiled forever."

"Ha!" Laura rolled her eyes. "Says the girl who once surfed in Hawaii!"

"Surfing Waimea Bay is completely different," Lynda replied. "I doubt Cancun gets twenty- or thirty-foot waves except maybe in a hurricane."

"That's fine with me," Amy said. "I don't want to see a tsunami."

"Not a tsunami," Cindi corrected. "Tsunamis are caused by disruption along the ocean floor…" She stopped. "Sorry. The teacher in me just comes out."

"That's all right." Jill looked out to sea. "There's lots we don't know about what lies under that water."

Dawn couldn't help but grin. "Sea monsters like Nessie in Scotland, maybe?"

"More likely Portuguese man o' war or eels or nettles, I'd guess," Sam said.

"Don't forget those giant rays and sharks of all sizes!"

"Ladies! If you keep talking, I'm pretty sure we're going to start hearing the theme song to *Jaws*." Sue laughed. "And then none of us are going to want to snorkel or swim."

"I had a friend who said a shark had come way too close to her once when she was scuba diving because she'd forgotten to take her engagement ring off."

"She's lucky the stone stayed in the setting, since the pressure changes fast," Lynda said, "but the shark was probably just attracted to the light refraction."

"*Just* attracted?" Dawn shivered. "I wouldn't want a shark attracted to me at all."

"They generally do not bother swimmers," Lynda said, "but yeah, I'd rather have had the guy on the next surfboard be attracted to me. Or..." She paused. "I would have when I was young."

"Forget about chronological age," Jill said. "We can be as young as we feel."

"Yeah, and if you like one of those guys out there, go for it," Dawn said. "You could be a mountain lion."

"I think you mean *cougar*," Cindi said. "Like on that TV show ten years ago."

Sue nodded. "Nothing wrong with an older woman picking up a younger guy."

Lynda grimaced. "I'm not looking for a younger guy. Or an older one, either."

Sam turned her gaze to the beach frolickers. A lot of them were young twenty-somethings, but there was certainly no absence of gray hair and bald heads. She'd always thought the beach was the greatest common denominator. It didn't matter what size or shape you were. The beach was a place to be shared by all.

But she didn't think that was what Lynda meant. Back in the summer before their senior year, a guy named Cliff Winslow had moved to Gainesbury from California. He'd been a surfer. A real one. Hitting the big waves off Malibu Beach. And he'd looked the part. All bronze-tan and hunky, with blond hair that fell over his eyes. Lynda had been smitten. They'd gotten married when they were just nineteen. Twenty years later, he'd left her for another woman, a much younger one.

Sam had lost touch with her several years later. She wondered now if Lynda was recalling her happier surfer days as she looked out over the water.

"Well," Jill said brightly as though she might be thinking the same thoughts about Lynda. "We are wasting the day standing here. Who wants to rent snorkels?"

****

As they sat down to dinner that night, all of them were sporting various shades of pink skin, a result of too much sun and not enough sun block.

"I'd forgotten how strong the sun is this far south, even in the winter," Cindi said. "I'm probably not going to get in the water at Cozumel tomorrow."

"Me either," Amy said, "I won't mind lounging in the shade of an umbrella, not at all, and reliving the movie we saw earlier."

When they'd returned to the ship, they had several hours before the late sitting for dinner and it was way too early for Happy Hour...or at least too early to start drinking this soon into the cruise. Maybe they'd all be sipping pina coladas for breakfast before it ended. However, the ship had a movie theater which had an early show for the late-seating diners and a late show for the early-seating ones. Since this cruise was Sixties-based and they had just had their first day on the beach, watching *Beach Party* seemed fitting.

"Funny how we were talking about being cougars and picking up a young guy earlier," Sue said, "and the movie was about the opposite... the older professor hitting on the teenager."

"*That* practice is still in force," Jill said, "and we *still* don't hear much criticism about a twenty-year age difference if it's the guy who's older."

This might be a touchy subject for Lynda. Sam glanced at her but couldn't tell from her expression. Still, "I think the point was that Frankie Avalon, the true boyfriend, wins back her attention in the end."

"But not before he does his own flirting with that foreign waitress," Dawn said.

"He was acting out of jealousy, of course," Jill answered.

"It's strange the games people play," Sue said.

Dawn giggled. "That reminds me of the country song about that."

Sam raised an eyebrow. "I didn't know you ever listened to anything but the British groups."

"Well, duh. They were my fave, but there were other groups I liked, too," Dawn replied. "Like, for instance, the songs in that movie we just watched. You can't get more American than that."

"Umm." Lynda looked pensive. "I remember a couple of lines from the country song you mentioned— something about not saying what they mean or meaning what they say." She shook her head. "I was so stupid about Cliff."

"You were a kid," Sue said. "We all were."

"Yeah, but the stupid stuff I did…how I acted…because I was obsessed with him…" She grimaced. "I'd never be such an idiot now."

Jill gave her a thoughtful look. "I think the movie provided a trigger for you. Do you want to talk about it?"

"No. Well…maybe." Lynda hesitated, then made a sound halfway between a laugh and a snort. "Well, why not, Dr. Jill? Maybe it'll be good to relive it and get it out of my system."

"Sometimes it does help," Jill replied. "And we are all ears."

****

Lynda's story: 1968

I remember looking at Laura practically in desperation as we sat on high stools at the soda fountain of the corner drug store, drinking our cherry cokes after school one day in late May. "I've tried everything to get Cliff's attention, and nothing seems to work."

Laura shook her head. "I find it hard to believe that *you*—probably the prettiest girl in our class—can't 'get your man.' Not that you're catty or even flirty, but you always seem to know what guys like to hear."

"I can hardly get close enough to talk to him." That was definitely part of the problem. Cliff Winslow had moved to Gainesbury from California—Malibu, to be exact—and he looked like the perfect surfer dude. Bronzed skin, sun-bleached hair, eyes the color of the sea, and a muscular body. He wasn't big and brawny like the football players and he wasn't lean like swimmers, but in the Levis and T-shirts he usually wore, he looked like he might have been sculpted out of stone. "Every girl in class is ape over him."

"Not me."

I remember rolling my eyes at her. "Of course not *you*. You've been going steady with Alexander for two years."

"Even if I weren't, Cliff's not my type," Laura replied. "I like tall, dark, and handsome. Maybe a little brooding, like Heathcliff. He's such a romantic, tormented anti-hero."

"That's because you're a drama queen," I replied. "And Heathcliff's character is about as opposite to the California beach culture as you can get."

Laura shrugged. "So, if he's into the beach and surfing, maybe you can follow him out to Galveston and ride the waves."

"Follow him? I have no idea when—or if—he's going to go there anytime soon." I frowned. "Besides, I'm not going to stalk the guy. That's too weird."

"I suppose you're right." Laura sighed. "Why don't you try the pool, then? It's opening for the summer this weekend. If he's there, you can show off your swimming skills and get his attention."

I studied her for a moment. "Maybe not a bad idea."

It seemed luck was with me the next day because when I got to the pool, I saw Cliff on the high board and watched as he executed a double somersault and then sliced the water cleanly. Maybe I should do a swan dive off the board, I thought. Just to show him I'm a serious athlete too.

But, as his head bobbed out of the water, some middle-school boys started rough-housing behind me. The lifeguard hollered at them to stop, but one of them managed to slide into me and I lost my balance and fell into the deep end. Because I'd been holding my suntan lotion and a towel, I floundered. The next thing I knew, strong arms were around me.

"Are you all right?" Cliff asked, making sure my head was above water.

And that's when the most stupid idea I've ever had hit me. Guys liked to rescue girls, right? At least, they did in the romance novels my mom liked to read. So…instead of being all athletic, maybe I should act just the opposite?

I gave him the most soulful look I knew how to do. "You saved my life!"

He blinked, then lifted me to the side of the pool before hoisting himself over the edge as well. "You don't know how to swim?"

"Well…" I couldn't lie, so I smiled disarmingly.

"You really shouldn't be at this end of the pool then," he said.

"I was watching you dive. You're really good."

"Thanks. I like the water." He looked at her. "Everyone should know how to swim. Do you want me to teach you the basics?"

How could I say no?

By the end of the afternoon, Cliff had taught me to jellyfish, back float, dog paddle, and even attempt the crawl. He seemed amazed at how quickly I caught on. I felt a little guilty about not letting him know I'd been the girls' swimming champ in junior high, but now that I had his undivided attention—he'd even asked me if I wanted to go to a movie that night—it just didn't seem the right time to bring it up…

****

Lynda sighed and looked over at Laura. "I remember you laughing your head off when I told you the next day."

"Well, it was a little hard to believe, since you had your lifeguard certification."

"Didn't you also have him 'teach' you to surf?" Dawn asked.

"Yeah. I even had to keep wiping out so he'd believe I didn't know a thing about being on a board." Lynda shook her head. "I can't believe I was willing to go to such lengths to catch the guy."

Laura patted her hand over the table. "You were as jazzed about him as I was about Alexander." She looked around at the group. "I suspect all of us did something silly or foolish."

"That we will hear about," Sam said. "At least Cliff isn't on board for the cruise."

"He probably knew better than to come," Laura said. "He turned out to be a real jerk, after all. Just like Alexander."

"And that," Sam said, "is another story."

Chapter Three

Stepping off their tender the next morning on Cozumel, Sam saw John Bond disembarking from another one, arriving just before them. She hadn't seen him yesterday, but there had been numerous places renting snorkel and scuba equipment. Or maybe he was one who didn't care to get sunburned by staying out on the beach. Not that it was her business. Today, though, he was dressed more casually in a polo shirt and khaki cargo shorts that revealed muscular calves. He was obviously one of those men who looked great in whatever they wore.

"Is that good-looking guy over there eyeing you?" Dawn asked as the rest of their group joined her.

"Probably not," she said just as he smiled and waved. "Well, maybe," she said as she waved back. "I met him briefly on the quay before boarding. His name is John Bond."

Sue raised an eyebrow. "*John* Bond?"

"I know. You think it should be James, right?"

"He *looks* like a James Bond," Laura said. "Actually, quite a bit like the tall, dark, and handsome one. He was the best."

"Yeah, he does look like him, but I don't think anyone played the role better than the actor who was slightly older, also dark and handsome, and maybe a little Scottish," Dawn said.

Laura laughed. "I was more a fan of the one who followed him. Loved the way he'd raise his eyebrows."

"Well, his name is John. John Bond. Not James." Sam turned to her friends and gave them a wry grin. "And he's the editor for *New Escapes* magazine, not an actor."

Jill looked over Sam's shoulder. "Whoever he is, he's coming this way."

"Mmmm. Lucky you," Dawn murmured. "He's dreamy."

Sam turned back to see him making his way across the crowded dock. "He's probably just going to ask us how we like the cruise so far, since he's doing research."

"Huh-uh. You can do *research* in a lot of ways." Dawn winked. "I wouldn't mind playing a role—"

"He could definitely have a leading role," Laura said.

"Oh, stop." Sam felt her face warming, and she was pretty sure it didn't have anything to do with the sun. Laura had been a real drama queen in high school. Not the kind who acted like a prima donna, but a real theater person. She'd played the lead in nearly every play the high school produced, including UIL—University Interscholastic League—one-act play competitions. She'd made a career operating and directing a little theatre, and it seemed she was still attuned to good-looking males who could play the lead man.

"Just saying," she replied.

Luckily, Laura didn't *say* anything more as he drew closer.

"Ladies." He gave a short bow to the group and then looked at Sam. "I was tied up in tele-conferences most of yesterday, but I've been hoping I'd spot you today."

"Oh?"

"Actually, I thought about what you said regarding your high school class celebrating its reunion with a cruise. It's an interesting idea and venue that might appeal to my magazine's readers. I was hoping you could spare me some time to share some of your experiences this week?"

Behind her, Laura made a sound that was suspiciously close to a quickly muffled laugh. She didn't dare look at her friend, although out of her peripheral vision she could see Dawn grinning and Sue smirking. Blast it! She felt her cheeks heat again and prayed John would think it was the sun. "I'd be glad to help."

"Fantastic." He glanced at the others before looking back to her. "I don't want to interrupt your plans with your friends—especially since this is a reunion—but could we meet for a drink in the Tiki lounge later this afternoon so we can make arrangements for the week?"

Behind her, that sound came from Laura again.

She lifted her chin slightly and smiled at John, trying to ignore the others, who were now practically gaping. "That will be fine. How about five o'clock?"

"Perfect. I'll meet you there then." He gave another nod to her friends, not indicating that he deemed their behavior a bit odd. "A pleasure, ladies."

"Ooooh," Dawn said as he left.

"Ahem." Laura cleared her throat. "Sounds like potential *research* to me."

Amy nodded. "He's definitely a hunk. Looks like you landed a good one."

"He's not a fish and I didn't *land* anyone." Sam said, wondering why her voice seemed to be pitched higher than usual. She coughed. "He probably just wants the perspective of a retiree to use for his magazine."

"Like you're the only retiree on this cruise?" Sue asked, smirking again.

"Of course not. I'm sure he'll be interviewing lots of people."

"He didn't ask any of the rest of us questions," Cindi pointed out.

"Just because—"

"You don't have to come up with reasons," Jill interrupted gently. "Why don't you just enjoy spending some time with him?" She was obviously using her psychologist's skills again. "Seize the moment."

"You are on a cruise, remember. They're supposed to be romantic," Dawn added.

Lynda snorted. "A shipboard romance probably won't last long."

"Whoa, guys. You practically have me married off to someone who simply wants to meet for a drink and ask some questions."

One corner of Laura's mouth quirked up. "It'll be interesting to find out how personal those questions will get."

Sam shook her head, knowing from past experience that Laura would go off the deep end—probably even as far as planning a wedding—if she didn't stop the flow of conversation right now.

"Let's explore Cozumel, shall we?"

****

"*Cozumel* means 'land of the swallows,' " the young lady who served as their tour guide said as she led their group away from the dock and onto an open-air vehicle that looked much like a giant dune buggy. It had several rows of wooden bench seats, the "sides" were only a railing, and there was a canvas top held up by four poles. Certainly not a bus, by American standards, but probably well-suited for a tropical island.

"There are over forty Mayan ruins on the island. It was considered a sanctuary where the Indians could hold ceremonies."

"What kind of ceremonies?" Jill asked.

"Originally, the native people worshiped Ixchel, the goddess of the moon."

Cindi smiled. "My name—Cynthia—means 'moon goddess' in Greek."

The guide gave her a quizzical look. "It does?"

"Well, in a roundabout way. Her Greek name is Artemis, but she was born on Mount Cynthus on Delos in the Cyclades."

The guide looked confused, and Sam intervened. "*Mi amiga es profesora de escuela.*"

The guide's expression lightened. "*¿Habla Español, Señora?*"

"*Hablo solo un poquito*…I speak only a little bit." She'd taken the language in high school since it was useful in Texas. And—in college—she and her friends would routinely take trips down to Reynosa or Nuevo Laredo and cross the border for a night of bar-hopping. Margaritas were only fifty cents and served by white-coated waiters who considered a quarter a huge tip. And—she cringed inwardly—she and her friends hadn't paid much attention to having a designated driver, either. Guardian angels were definitely underrated. She turned her thoughts away from how foolish they had all been.

"So…" the guide was saying as their vehicle swayed to a stop in front of a low, square building of coral slabs that sat on a plot of loose sand surrounded by palm trees and jungle vegetation. It had a tiered roof and another smaller replica of itself on the very top. "…this is *el Templo del Caracol*. It is a temple to honor Ixchel." As they clambered down to explore the inside, she added, "The shells on the roof make a whistling sound when the winds grow strong. It was said Ixchel was protecting her people by letting them know a great storm approached."

That was most likely myth, but it did add to the ambiance of the small, plain building set in an isolated area.

"An early hurricane warning system," Laura said, a look of awe on her face. "And how old is it?"

"Perhaps a thousand years." The guide shrugged. "Or a bit more modern."

By "a bit" did she mean a couple of hundred years *newer*? Sam watched as Laura narrowed her eyes speculatively and studied the interior. It was an expression she used when she was contemplating setting up a scene.

"The lighting is very interesting in here."

Or perhaps an entire play was developing in Laura's mind. Of all of them, she had the strongest imagination. Sam could almost see her recruiting some of the local cabana boys to serve as willing slaves to a beautiful moon goddess chosen from the local girls, once they got back to the beach.

"Ah, Laura, if you're thinking what I think you're thinking, I doubt the Mayans would appreciate your disturbing this place."

Laura frowned at her. "You don't think thousands of tourists haven't already done that?" She looked around again. "This really would make for a lovely, surreal video I could post on YouTube."

"No. Besides, I'm pretty sure you'd need permission from the Mexican government to do something like that."

"Umm." Laura sounded noncommittal.

The last thing they needed was to be arrested by the local authorities. Long gone were the days when such a thing might be an adventure to be talked about. "We all want to just enjoy the cruise…and finish it in Galveston like we're supposed to."

"Umm," Laura said again.

Sam groaned. Since the ship wasn't sailing until dusk, that meant Laura would have the whole afternoon to launch her shenanigans. She needed to be back on board by five o'clock to meet John, which meant the rest of them would have to keep an eye on their friend.

Or they might well be sailing without her.

****

"So you did return to the ship," Sam said as she slipped into her chair next to Laura at dinner later that night.

"Of course I did." Laura looked disgruntled. "What else could I do? I had six guards surrounding me the whole time."

"We weren't *guards*," Cindi said.

"No?" Laura looked around the table. "We probably looked like we were tied together with an invisible rope. I couldn't even wander off to shop."

"We shopped together," Jill said. "You got some very nice things."

Laura slanted her a look. "Are you trying to use your psycho training on me?"

"Maybe."

"Anyway, no one got arrested. " Amy, the practical

one, moved them away from an argument. "We're all safely back on board."

"And I want to know how your date with John went," Sue said, changing the subject completely.

Sam shook her head. "It wasn't a *date*. Just a meeting."

"To-*may*-to, to-*mah*-to." Sue wagged a finger. "Stop dealing in semantics. You *meet* when you're on a date, don't you?"

"It was *drinks*."

"Drinks? With an 's'?" Dawn asked. "How many did you have?"

She shook her head. Obviously, her friends were not going to give up until they squeezed every drop of information out of her. "Two each—"

"Aha!" Sue exclaimed. "If the guy bought you two drinks, it means—"

"It *means* we were taking up a table while he was outlining his project," Sam said firmly. "Waiters rely on tips, you know. They don't want people sitting at one of their tables not ordering anything for a couple of hours."

"A couple of hours?" Dawn's eyes widened. "If you spent a couple of hours, he must really like you."

"He was giving me his ideas for the article he wants to do." She hesitated, bracing herself for the barrage of questions that surely would follow her next statement. "He's thinking about extending it into a series of articles—he sends one to his office in New York each night—and was wondering if it would be all right if he accompanied us on some of the excursions—"

"I *knew* it!" Dawn nearly bounced in her seat. "He's really into you!"

"If you'll let me finish! He said that way he'd be

able to observe *all* of us and ask questions and get a better idea of marketing cruises for women travelling alone."

"*And* he'd be able to spend more time with you," Sue said slyly.

Sam felt her cheeks warm and hoped her sunburn would cover the color. She couldn't deny she'd enjoyed his attention, but she definitely didn't want to give her friends ideas. "He didn't imply that."

Dawn rolled her eyes. "Do you expect him to spell it out? Maybe he's being subtle."

"And sneaky."

All eyes turned to Laura as she made that remark. She shrugged, looked away, and then turned back. "Sam doesn't know this guy. None of us do. He's good-looking, obviously suave and sophisticated, a smooth talker—"

"I think Sam's smart enough not to be taken in," Amy said.

"Unless she wants to be," Jill added.

"It doesn't hurt to flirt a little if you're single," Cindi said.

"It doesn't," Laura replied. "And it doesn't hurt to look, either. Heck, I was doing it too. I'm just saying be careful so you don't get burned." She paused. "You do remember what happened to me in high school, don't you?"

****

Laura's story: 1969

We'd just returned from Christmas break and Buzz Newton was late for seventh-period English class. Again. All female eyes turned to the door as he entered, in no apparent hurry. He grinned at the teacher as he put a pass on her desk and then winked at one of the girls in the front row as he took his seat. She blushed and a couple of other girls gave him hopeful smiles.

Apparently word had already gotten out that he'd broken up with me over the holidays.

I remember keeping my head down and pretending to be interested in Chaucer's *Canterbury Tales*. The teacher had told us to read it and be ready to discuss it tomorrow. I had no clue what it was about except I was grateful it wasn't Elizabeth Barrett Browning. I didn't need any reminders about how many ways I loved—had loved—him.

We'd been going steady for two years, and Buzz was everything I wanted. He was cute and popular and we were always invited to the right parties. Half the girls in senior class would die to go out with him. And he was mine. Or at least I thought he was.

I'd spent most of the holidays in a deep funk, bursting into tears every time "I Heard It Through the Grapevine" came on my transistor radio.

Lynda had called the first Sunday of vacation and asked if Buzz and I had had a fight. I said no, we never fought. Now I realize that was because I always gave in to him, but at the age of seventeen, I was so blown away by him that it didn't even occur to me. I asked why, and she'd hesitated. Then she tried to sound casual when she said she'd seen him and Annie Smith at the pizza parlor the night before. I remember telling Lynda that Buzz had said he was going over to help Annie's brother work on his car and that's probably why they'd all gone out for a pizza. The phone was quiet for so long, I'd wondered if Lynda had hung up. But then she told me quietly that Annie's brother hadn't been with them.

"Hey. You all right?"

I blinked, coming out of my doldrums, and looked at Rod Talman, sitting across the aisle from me.

"Yeah, I'm fine." If you could call someone fine who was about to completely lose it right there in the classroom. "I…I'm reading."

He didn't say anything else and I was grateful. Rod was a nice guy, kind of quiet and always polite and respectful. I kept flipping pages unseeingly until he reached over and gently pulled the book from me and closed it.

"That was the bell," he said with a smile. "You aren't planning to spend the night here, are you?"

"Oh," I said stupidly and gathered my books. At least Buzz was gone.

Rod walked with me to my locker, talking about basketball and the big game with our opponent next week. I suspect he was trying to keep me from wallowing in self-pity. He was sensitive that way and no doubt had heard the breakup news too.

And then it happened.

Buzz walked by, looked once, then twice, and took a step back.

"Well, Roddy, old boy. Aren't you kind of a fast worker?" He gave me a glance. "Or maybe she is?"

My cheeks burned. He was the one who'd cheated on me. How could he be so mean? I grabbed my coat and hurried down the hall and down the steps to the first floor. I heard Rod call after me, but I didn't stop.

Once outside, I started running. Not in the direction of home, though. I needed to be by myself. Needed to get away. I ran and ran. Blindly.

Finally, exhausted, I slowed to a walk. I was out on

the highway on the edge of town, and dusk had already fallen. I knew I should go home, but I kept on walking.

Cars zoomed past, a couple of drivers honking their horns at me to get off the road. And then a car slowed and pulled over. I didn't recognize the car or the driver. It was too dark. My heart stood still and I wanted to run, but my feet wouldn't move. The road was suddenly deserted. Where was the traffic?

I heard a car door slam and then footsteps. My brain re-engaged and I started to run, not looking back. Adrenaline must have kicked in, because I caught a second wind.

I didn't see the pothole until it was too late. My ankle turned and I went down.

"Laura!" Suddenly, Rod was hunched down beside me. "Why did you run?"

"I…didn't know who you were. I thought…" I shuddered. How many times had my parents told me it wasn't safe on the roads at night? "I mean—"

"I'm sorry for scaring you. I went to your house to make sure you got home okay, since you seemed sort of out-of-it at school. Your mom said you hadn't gotten back yet. Then I had to get my dad's car, and I really didn't know where to start looking…" He stopped. "Are you hurt?"

"I… I don't think so." I moved my foot, thankful it seemed to be okay. "I acted pretty stupid, didn't I?"

He didn't answer that question, not that he needed to. "Let's get you home," he said instead.

I stared out the window for a few minutes after we'd gotten back to the car, and then I turned to Rod. "I really messed up, didn't I?"

He gave me a glance, then turned his attention back

to the road. "I don't think anything was your fault."

"I guess you heard about Buzz and me breaking up?"

He gave me another quick glance. "Yes. The guy's a real…" He clamped his mouth shut. "Look. I know it's too soon to even bring this up, but maybe—when you feel better—we could go out for a coke or something? Maybe get to know each other better?"

"Umm—"

"Don't answer me now. It can wait." He pointed. "Besides, you're home."

The porch light was on at my place, and the door opened when Rod pulled into the driveway. My mother hurried down the drive.

"Thank goodness you're okay! Dad has been out looking for you."

I cringed a little as I got out of the car. I was going to have some big explaining to do once he got home. I turned back to Rod.

"I'm pretty sure I'm going to be grounded for the rest of my life, but—just in case I'm not—that coke date sounds great to me."

****

Sam looked around the group as Laura finished her story. Lynda actually had tears in her eyes. Not too surprising, since they'd been best friends. But then Lynda wiped them away and smiled.

"At least you had a happy ending."

"For sure." Laura gave them all a grin. "I married Rod, after all."

Chapter Four

More than a dozen old-style school buses were lined up the next morning as groups of passengers stepped off the tenders once more in Cancun. John Bond had joined their group to board one of them.

Although he had greeted all her friends, Sam still could sense their hidden smirks and overly curious gazes as he stood beside her. Really? How many times did she need to reiterate that the man was gathering material for a magazine article, not coming on to her?

A large group of soldiers emerged from the station house as the tourists began boarding. They were in full military gear, including assault rifles and wicked-looking daggers attached to ammunition belts.

"I wonder if they're going to check us for weapons or drugs?" she asked.

"Doubtful," John answered. "They're for protection."

"Protection?"

"It's about eighty miles from here to Tulum," he replied, "and we'll be travelling through heavy jungle part of the way."

"Are drug cartels likely to waylay us? They do know that's not good for tourism, right?"

"They do and, for the most part, they don't see any value in attacking a bunch of tourists, but just to make sure, the Mexican government sends a warning by putting soldiers on the buses." He shrugged. "But there are also ragged bands of banditos who may be hungry or desperate enough to try highjacking a bus. It's another reason why the tour companies travel in caravans."

That explanation brought some serious expressions to her friends' faces. Their two previous days had been carefree, on sandy white beaches, with cabana boys carrying tropical drinks to sunbathers, and mariachi music in the background. Today, they were actually going to go into Mexico, albeit along the eastern coast line.

It probably didn't help that the soldiers looked equally grim. They obviously weren't there for public relations, since not one of them cracked a smile and most had their fingers alongside the triggers on their rifles.

Once on board, though, a cheerful young man, dressed in the traditional white Guayabera shirt, greeted them like they were long-lost relatives and offered them chilled *cerveza* from a cooler by the driver's seat. Although it was a little early to be drinking beer, Sam figured maybe the tour company felt the passengers would forget about the armed guards if they were a little blitzed.

However, once the bus turned off the main road and down a single-lane, rutted dirt road winding through the dense brush, she realized the bus didn't have any springs. It might have had, originally, but if so, they were long worn out. Being jostled about on the thinly padded seats wasn't exactly helping her bladder, and from the looks on her friends' faces, they were having a similar problem.

"More *cerveza*?" the young guide, whose name tag declared him to be Jose, asked as he walked down the swaying aisle. He'd obviously done this many times, since he deftly managed not to bounce against any seats.

"*No, gracias,*" she answered as her friends shook their heads.

Jose's face fell, and Sam was tempted to take another beer just not to insult him. But there was going to be a serious problem with the slacks she wore if she did.

"The cerveza was good," she said instead, "but a bit early in the morning for more than one, *¿no?*"

"*Si,*" he replied, but he looked puzzled, as though he didn't understand why someone wouldn't want to drink in the middle of the morning. Maybe he chalked it up to *Americanos locos* or maybe his English was limited.

Beside her, John chuckled. "At least we can't complain about his hospitality."

"That's true," she said, squirming a little and hoping John wouldn't realize why.

"Not quite a luxury coach, is it?" he asked.

She dipped her head in acknowledgement. "I've been on worse methods of transport, though."

"Oh?" He looked interested. "Don't tell me you went on a trek on the veldt in Africa, or maybe rode a camel in the Mideast?"

"No camels." She smiled. "Horses, mules, donkeys, though. Once even a dog sled. All in the line of duty, of course."

"Really?" An eyebrow lifted. "What was it you did? Work as a secret agent for the FBI or CIA?"

"Not quite. Although I did work for the government. I was a Parks and Wildlife ranger."

He asked more questions, and soon she was regaling him with some of the funnier things that had happened in her career. When the bus jolted to a stop, she was surprised to find out they were at Tulum.

"Good God. Have I been talking all this time?"

"I enjoyed it," John said. "You are a very interesting person."

****

As they ducked through the stone arch of the ancient wall around Tulum, Sam straightened and gasped involuntarily. Before her, in the space of about a quarter of an acre, lay an entire Mayan city. Much of it was in ruins, but the magnificent "castle" with its dozens of steep steps leading to the first platform was intact and dominated the entire area.

"*Es muy grande, ¿no?*" Jose, who was also going to be their guide, asked as he came up beside her.

"*Si.*" She looked around again. "It is amazing to think something like that was built without modern technology or forklifts and cranes."

Jose nodded. "Some buildings are twenty-five hundred years old."

"And the oldest structures in the United States might date back to the middle 1600s," she said. "Of course, we have pueblo ruins in the West that were built in the late twelfth century, but still not as old as this."

The others gathered around them, and Jose pointed to his left. "What you see in front of you are platforms that formed houses for the common people." He waved his hand to the right. "And close to that wall is another bigger one." He gestured to two structures in front of them. "The one on your right is a tomb, the one on the left is the House of Chultun, or House of Water." He pointed once more to his left. "And by the far wall is the House of Cenote, which was built over a cave that also

44

collected water."

"Like a well?" someone asked.

"*Si*. It was originally used for drinking, but it has now become too salty."

"We forget how primitive things were. It's a wonder humankind survived," Sam said.

"Well, this would be the place they did," Jose answered. "Tulum was built to honor the god Itzamna."

"Who was?"

"The god of the earth and all living things. Legend has it he was married to Ixchel—"

"The moon goddess from Cozumel?"

"*Si*. Together they had many children and created humankind."

"So this could be another Garden of Eden."

"I suppose it could be." Jose gave her a thoughtful look. "Perhaps you can decide when we are finished."

As they started to walk toward the castle, Jose pointed out more tombs and shrines, stopping again midway. "The ruins on your left are the House of Columns, or the palace," he said. "Next to the castle, it was the largest structure in the city." He turned slightly toward an intact building with a gallery over the first floor and an additional, smaller building on top of that. "The Temple of the Frescos," he said, "is at the direct center of the city."

He continued to describe other structures as they followed him—rather like baby ducks—as they circled the area. On the southeast corner, he pointed out the Temple to the Sea and on the northeast corner stood the Temple to the Wind.

"We got a glimpse of that when we drove up," another person said. "It looked magnificent from the road."

"*Si*. There is a beach you can walk to and get a really good picture," Jose said. "But it is a pretty steep incline and there are loose rocks, so you have to be careful."

"Will we have time?" Sam asked.

Jose grinned. "In Mexico, we believe in *manana*, meaning we are in no hurry. The bus drivers get a longer *siesta* if we linger, no?"

That brought a laugh from everyone and they scattered to explore on their own. Sam elected to make her way down to the beach and was pleasantly surprised when John decided to accompany her. He stayed close, catching her elbow once when her foot slipped and another time descending a two-foot drop first to help her down.

"Thank you," she said.

"No need," he answered. "I wouldn't want you to hurt yourself."

She was about to remind him that she had been a park ranger and used to hiking uneven trails, but managed to clamp her mouth shut before the words came out.

It had been a long time since a man actually had acted like he cared.

****

It was rather ironic that "I Want To Hold Your Hand" was playing over the PA system when her group gathered in the Oasis Lounge prior to dinner that night. Not that John had actually held her hand for any length of time on their descent to the beach earlier, but his taking her hand to help her along the trail—heavens, she hoped she hadn't acted like a damsel-in-distress—had evoked a warm, cozy feeling inside her.

In an absurd way, it had also reminded her of the night she'd almost killed Jack. Once he'd recovered from having a shotgun aimed at him, he'd insisted on walking her sister and herself home, and *he* had taken her hand so she wouldn't slip on the muddy trails. Her sister had snickered at the time and run on ahead.

She looked at the stage that dominated the far end of the dining room. It had a British flag draped in the background and four young men, sporting mop-tops and dressed in iconic collarless suits took their spots.

"It looks like the British are going to invade us again," she said as they began to play "Yesterday."

"Are you trying to distract us?" Sue asked.

She didn't need to ask what Sue meant. Her friends were watching her like cats at a mousehole. Sam sighed. "Before you ask, John did not make a pass at me this afternoon."

"Doesn't mean he didn't want to," Sue said.

"That's true." Cindi nodded. "He wouldn't want to make a spectacle of himself with other people around."

"Especially considering he's on business," Laura added.

"Will you guys stop!" Sam shook her head. "Honestly, you all remind me of Julie McCoy, the cruise director on *Love Boat*. 'Romance' is *not* in the air."

"Umm." Dawn looked skeptical. "The lady doth protest too much, me thinks."

Sam smiled. "You're quoting Shakespeare now?"

"Well, you know I've always loved everything British."

"God knows that's true," Lynda said. "Half the time the rest of us couldn't understand your British slang— like calling Jack O'Neill a bovver boy."

Laura laughed. "For once, he didn't know what to say, because he didn't know if you were insulting him or not."

"That was up to him to decide, I guess," Dawn replied, " since it meant someone young who causes or seeks out trouble."

"I'm pretty sure he'd have taken that as a compliment," Sam said.

"Probably," Jill said, "but I also remember Dawn trying to sound like British royalty, too."

"I was pretty affected, wasn't I?" Dawn laughed. "I couldn't decide if I wanted to be a common bird that the blokes liked or—" She lifted her nose and sniffed. "—a member of the aristocracy."

"It's a good thing the Prince was still in high school when we were," Jill said, "and didn't have any serious girlfriends yet."

Laura lifted an eyebrow. "Well, as mesmerized as everyone has been with *The Crown* series, I'd say interest in the aristocracy still continues."

"Actually, any aristocracy is intriguing in its own way," Sam said. "We saw the remnants of an ancient aristocracy today at the ruins."

"True." Cindi looked thoughtful. "The Mayans had a hierarchy, too. I read up on it before we left. A king, nobles—who included the high priests—warriors next, then craftsmen and merchants, and finally the laborers and farmers."

"It's rather a pity that farmers and laborers are always at the bottom of the list," Amy said, "considering if it weren't for their efforts, the nobility wouldn't have anything to eat or anyone to do the work."

Jill nodded. "And people were relegated to their own

class. It was hard to improve their lot in the world."

"In spite of Regency romances having dukes marrying girls from Covent Garden?" Sue teased.

Jill gave her a wry smile. "I doubt that *ever* happened in real time. It wasn't so much that the aristocrats intentionally were snobs, but they were inherently taught that they were a class of their own."

"Good thing you didn't give yourself airs." Lynda gave Dawn a playful poke. "Or we wouldn't have been allowed to speak to you."

Instead of laughing with the rest of them, Dawn's expression turned serious. "You know, I'm ashamed to say this, but I really was a snob once."

As puzzlement grew on their faces, Sam asked. "When?"

"It was with my cousin. None of you ever met her." Dawn grimaced. "I really wasn't very nice."

Sam paused. "Do you want to talk about it?"

Dawn took a deep breath. "Even after these years, it still bothers me that I acted like I did, so I think I need to."

****

Dawn's story: 1966

"Dawn!" Mom called as I came home from school, "there's a letter for you on the hall table."

Letter? I laid down my books and went over to read it. "Oh, no," I moaned to myself as I raced through it. It was from my cousin Trudy, and she was inviting me to come to California for Spring Break. Her letter was wildly enthusiastic about all the *fun* we'd have and the cute dates she'd line up for me...or so she planned.

Well, I thought, I just can't go. Not with the Sweetheart Ball being held this Saturday. I had other things lined up, too. And, besides, I *remembered* Trudy!

She was everything square and un-cool. The last time I'd seen her must have been three years earlier, but I still had a vivid picture of a pudgy, freckled face and carrot-colored hair that stuck out at all angles. She had a shrill laugh that sounded like a cat had gotten its tail pinched under a rocker, and she was *loud*.

"Who is the letter from, dear?" my mother asked as she walked into the hall.

"Uh…" I started. "Oh… It's from Trudy."

"Well, that's nice," Mom said brightly. 'You haven't heard from her for ages. She was always such a sweet little girl. What does she want?"

Sweet little girl? How offbeat can a parent get anyhow? I almost forgot to answer. When she asked again, I handed her the letter. She read it slowly and thoughtfully. Watching her, I had a suspicion something was coming. Then she dropped the bombshell. I nearly fell out of my tree.

"What are you going to take along?"

"Take along?" I tried not to shriek. "Mother! I'm not going. There's this dance, and my new dress, and you know how I like Rich Johnson. He said he'd see me there."

"If Rich wanted to see you there, he should have asked you to be his date," my mother said firmly. "You are not going to refuse this invitation, dance or not. There will be others. You haven't seen Trudy for years. It wouldn't be polite to refuse." She handed the letter back. "Now, let's hear no more about it."

I watched her go back to the kitchen, trying to think of something drastic to do. I had a huge urge to stomp my foot like a child or, better, throw a tantrum, but then

I thought about the with-it girls like Twiggy and Jean Shrimpton and tossed my head. I rushed up the stairs instead, trying not to cry until I was safely inside my room. I slammed the door and flopped on the bed, totally miserable.

To argue would be useless…at least, when my mother had "that look" on her face. Instead of dancing with Rich, I would be spending the weekend with Trudy and her dorky friends. What a bummer. I'd be lucky if the "date" she'd lined up didn't look like one of the Munsters.

It just wasn't fair, I told myself, wallowing in self-pity.

I complained about it all week, at home, at school, even to Rich. All anyone said was *Maybe she's changed…* or *Think of the warm California sun and all those beach boys.* Even Rich said something about enjoying the beach. A lot he cared if I met any cute guys. Not that I expected Trudy to know any.

Mom helped me pack or, at least, she started to. I told her exactly what I thought of the whole mess. I told her how I'd feel the whole weekend…miserable because my friends would be having fun here while I was with Trudy and some of her boring friends. And, to put good measure to it, I sarcastically added, "Doesn't that sound just fab? Really gear?"

I remember my mother looking at me sadly. "Trudy isn't as bad as all that. Your whole outlook on this matter could use a little adult thinking. You act like such a baby. Maybe this weekend will do you some good." Then she walked out, leaving me staring after her.

When my well-meaning older brother drove me to the airport, he said the same thing, only more bluntly.

"For Pete's sake, Dawn, get a hold of yourself. Do you think the world was made for you alone? Well, think twice. Whatever you do, don't let Trudy know what you're thinking. She might want to strangle you, and right now, I'm thinking of doing that myself."

With those cheerful words, and my mother's "advice" ringing in my ears, I boarded my flight. On the way, I gave some serious thought to what my family had said. I guess my friends had been trying to tell me the same thing. I resolved to act like there was nothing wrong with Trudy. Maybe I could even fake enjoyment on a date or two.

I certainly wasn't ready for the sight that greeted my eyes when I collected my luggage and went outside to the curb to wait for Trudy. There was a tall, slim girl dressed in mod clothes, with go-go boots and long, blonde-streaked straight hair, standing by a parked convertible. She was surrounded by four of the best-looking hunks I'd ever seen. They all seemed absolutely delighted by her, and I wondered if she were an English model. I watched her wistfully, wishing I could be in her place, while waiting for Trudy and her mom to come. Not that I had ever been able to keep four guys focused on me. But she was really out-of-sight.

Just then, she turned and saw me. With a bright smile, she waved. "Hi, Dawn! Remember me?"

****

"I really was such a snob, just like those aristocrats we were talking about." Dawn grimaced when she'd finished her story. "I really was ashamed of myself."

"It was probably a valuable lesson," Jill said. "Sometimes it takes my patients years of therapy to discover something like that."

"Yeah, yeah. Lesson learned," Sue said. "But if I remember correctly, one of those guys started writing to you afterwards."

"Jason. He looked like he belonged in a British band, and he could sing, too. I thought maybe I was going to be dating a rock star. He went on to college and got a doctorate in aerospace engineering instead. Just goes to show that we shouldn't be judging people by their looks." She quirked her mouth. "I finally grew up, I guess."

Chapter Five

Standing on deck, Sam looked out over sparkling turquoise waters and a white streak of sand that looked like it was lying atop the waves. They'd crossed the Gulf of Mexico during the night and gone from an ancient Mayan temple perched on a tall sea cliff to a partially finished American fortress on a flat island with a high elevation of ten feet.

"Fort Jefferson," John said as he joined our group waiting for the next tender to shore. "Did you know it was never fully armed?"

"I didn't." Sam looked at her friends. "Did any of you?" When they all shook their heads, she turned back to John. "Do you know its history?"

"Some. It originally was intended to protect the Florida Straits from pirates, but it's also a strategic location to ward off foreign enemies. Construction started in 1846, but because of the massive number of bricks that had to be hauled in, it took thirty years to build. By that time, military battle equipment had changed and the rifled cannon made it nearly useless as an actual fort."

Sue snorted. "Seems our government was wasting taxpayer money even then."

Not wanting to get the group involved in politics— their views had always run the gamut from really liberal to very conservative—Sam looked at John.

"Was researching the history of the fort a personal interest?"

He shook his head. "I did an article on the Dry Tortugas for my magazine last year. The isolation— seventy miles from Key West—and the lack of tourists appeal to some of our readers who don't want to mingle with the sunbaked crowds." He gave them a self-deprecating grin. "Since it was once used as a prison, I guess you could say those folks got their wish."

Sam raised an eyebrow. "I assume those clients didn't actually get to reside as guests?"

His grin widened. "No. The fort housed Civil War prisoners, a bit before our current clientele were around." He sobered as he looked across the water at a side of the hexagonal-shaped building. "Dr. Samuel Mudd was one of the prisoners."

"The physician who tended John Wilkes Booth?" Amy asked.

"Yes. His Hippocratic Oath didn't make a difference in accusing him of aiding and abetting an assassin," he answered. "Of course, it may have been a blessing in disguise, since there were a number of other soldiers— mainly deserters and such—there at the time, and Yellow Fever was rampant."

Amy shuddered. "I'm glad we've come a long way to wiping out those diseases. Modern medicine is a miracle, too."

Sam smiled at her. Amy was a veterinarian. "I suppose you're including your four-legged patients in that?"

"Of course." She looked puzzled. "Why wouldn't I?"

Sam had almost forgotten how much Amy had

always loved animals. To her friend, they were humans with fur. Or feathers. Visiting her back when they were in school had always meant being assailed by a half-dozen dogs and removing cat hair from clothes later…not to mention dodging a dive-bombing parakeet and trying to be heard over the chattering of dozens of squirrels who competed with squawking, indignant mockingbirds, crackles, and jays at the birdfeeders just off the patio. She even remembered a duck with a broken wing one time. Amy had put out a child's inflatable swimming pool for it until it recovered. She smiled again.

"I suspect you have done your own research since the Tortugas are supposed to be a bird-watching paradise."

Amy's eyes sparkled as she smiled back. "I have. This was the place I was most looking forward to. Did you know there are over three hundred different species of birds who nest here?" Ignoring several subtle groans, she went on. "Masked boobies, peregrine falcons, yellow-billed cuckoos…" Warming up to her subject, her voice rose a bit. "Did you know that a female sooty tern only has one offspring a year?"

It didn't seem to matter that no one answered and, blessedly, no one rolled their eyes, either. Not that Amy would have noticed, probably. Once she was into lecture mode, she stayed focused.

"That species nests on Bush Key, which is why no one is allowed there. I wish I had brought binoculars. Maybe then…" She sighed. "Well, anyway, we should be able to spot a frigate bird, since their wing span reaches seven feet."

"You're quite knowledgeable," John said. "Are you

aware of the different species of fish as well?"

"Not so much," she answered, "although I do have a salt-water aquarium at home. Tangs, mostly, with some blue damsels and clownfish."

"Ernest Hemingway used to come out here to do sports fishing back in the 1930s," John said. "Of course, he and his friends were seeking somewhat larger fish, like amberjack, tarpon, and swordfish."

Amy frowned. "I certainly hope it was catch-and-release only."

John hesitated. "I…am not sure."

"Hemingway was a hunter, too, wasn't he?"

"Ah…" He must have realized he was venturing into dangerous territory. "I…guess so. I don't normally research people, though."

Amy looked as though she were about to launch into another lecture, and Sam breathed a sigh of relief when a crew member approached to let them know the tender was waiting for their group to go to the island.

Exploring the fort—even if it were fully armed with cannons pointing at them and soldiers at the ready—would be preferable to facing Amy's wrath when she got started on protecting animals.

"Well, come on, then," she said, taking Amy's arm. "Let's see if we can find a nice iguana for you to pet."

****

The theme for the evening was a tribute to *Star Trek*. At the door to the dining room, an easel held a large poster of the *USS Enterprise* with the caption politically corrected to read, "…boldly go where no one has gone before." Sam felt her mouth quirk. Someone from HR had no doubt decided the change would be appropriate to make any Women's Libber aboard the ship proud.

Laser beams in soft shades of blue, green, and pink flashed across the ceiling of the dining room as Sam entered accompanied by "A Place in the Sun," which she supposed was apropos, considering the starship explored the universe.

"Care for a tribble?" Sue asked as Sam joined their table.

She took the furry little blob from Sue and sat down, petting it instinctively. "I hope you haven't fed it, since they tend to reproduce after a meal."

Sue gestured toward several more on the table. "I think that's already been done."

"No. The crew just created a centerpiece of them so everyone at the table would get one," Amy said, stroking her own little furball. It emitted a soothing coo sound, and she looked surprised. "Wow. They even imitated the sound from the show."

Sam laughed. "I guess that means there aren't any Klingons around. If I remember correctly, the tribbles hated them."

"For good reason," Amy answered. "The Klingons wanted to destroy their planet."

"Well." Sue looked around. "It seems the wait staff are on our side."

Sam followed her gaze. Last night, the waiters had been decked out in London-mod jackets. Tonight, they wore costume tops in either yellow, blue, or red, depending on which sector they were supposedly representing. Each had its iconic inverted V emblem over the heart. She frowned slightly. Captain Kirk, Mr. Spock, Scotty, and Bones were markedly absent, as were Chekov, Uhura, and Sulu. "I don't see the main players, though."

Sue pointed to a stage that tonight had what looked like clear plastic tubes standing on it. "I suspect they'll beam in for a show later."

"Hmmm." Jill contemplated the stage setting. "I wonder how long it will be before science will allow us to transport like that."

Dawn shuddered. "Never, I hope. Imagine what would happen if your cells—or whatever—got mixed up and you came out looking like someone else."

"I think you're confusing *Star Trek* with a movie that did that," Amy said.

"Oh, yes, and it was a horrible movie! I had nightmares about it." Dawn maintained her serious expression. "I, for one, will not get into any kind of machine."

Sue lifted an eyebrow. 'Didn't you fly here? In a plane?"

Dawn drew her own brows together. "Of course I did. I drive a car, too, but you know what I mean."

"Well, we probably don't have to worry about it anytime soon," Laura said.

Jill gave her a contemplative look. "I'm not so sure. Look at the stuff they used on *Star Trek*. Handheld computers…wireless speaker devices…stuff that seemed really far-out in the Sixties. These days we all have tablets and cell phones."

"Don't forget that one movie—where Scotty sits down and speaks to the computer, expecting it to answer. At the time, I thought that was one of the funniest lines I'd ever heard." Amy shrugged. "Now we have artificial intelligence that actually does that."

"And we can see each other on our phones and computers, too," Jill added. "That was something else that was unheard of back then."

"Okay. If we really want to show our age," Lynda said, "remember when the internet didn't exist? We were all wondering how something called 'the world-wide-web' could actually work."

They were interrupted by a waiter who handed out menus appropriately titled "Ship's Log" for the evening. Sam smiled as she scanned the items with adjectives such as "star-glazed" and "intergalactic-iced" added.

"I'm not sure of some of these concoctions," she said, "but I assume everything is designed for human consumption."

Amy glanced at the tribble beside her plate. "Unless maybe…"

They all laughed.

"Let's not go there," Sam said. "You remember what happened in the show. The crew was overcome by them."

"Maybe I could write a story about tribbles," Cindi said. "My publisher is always asking for new ideas."

"You'd better stick with something safe, like a puppy story," Jill answered. "After all, with all the things we never thought would come to fruition actually doing so, maybe we shouldn't tempt fate."

Amy nodded. "I like puppy stories."

Dawn gave her an indulgent look. "You like any kind of animal story."

"I guess that's true enough."

"You've always had a soft spot for both people and animals. I think the gods rewarded you with both a great career and a super-wonderful husband," Sam said.

"One who couldn't be here because his surgery schedule is full," Amy replied, "but that's one thing we've always understood about each other. There are priorities greater than our own wants."

"Not everyone was so lucky as you," Dawn said.

Sam gave her a quick look. Her divorce—while not as traumatic as Lynda's—hadn't been particularly amiable, but then she wondered if anyone's was. But best not to get maudlin. "And some of us didn't marry at all."

"You wouldn't have married Jack even if he'd asked," Sue said tartly.

Sam felt herself flush and hoped the light was low enough so no one would notice. "Jack? Good grief. Would you have married him?"

"No," Sue answered, "but I wasn't the one who constantly sparred with him over everything, either."

Jill looked amused. "Some couples do show their love by bickering."

"Hmph." Sam gave an unladylike snort. "I prefer to keep my stress level down. Besides, we weren't talking about me. We were telling Amy how lucky she was to have landed Jim."

"Or maybe, *he* was the lucky one," Cindi said.

"We were both lucky…and blessed." Amy looked a little pensive. "And to think it almost didn't happen."

Sam squinted her eyes. "That's right. If I remember correctly, you were all gaga over that Paul guy."

Amy rolled her eyes. "Stupid me. Would you believe I actually cried over that jerk before I came to my senses?"

"You did?"

"Yes." She shook her head. "In retrospect, I suppose maybe the gods did intervene. Do you want to hear about it?"

"Why not?" Sam looked at the rest of them. "We all

are supposed to share a story this week. So what is Amy's to be?"

****

Amy's story: 1968

The Junior-Senior prom was only one week away and I didn't have a date yet. I had pretty much decided I wasn't going. I really wanted to scratch the eyes out of Michelle Porter, a certain southern-drawling redhead. If she hadn't moved to Gainesbury, I'd be going to the prom with Paul.

Paul Scottero. A six-foot hunk with coal black hair and eyes almost as dark. He had an engaging grin, could really dance, and was considered quite the catch. His family owned a popular pizzeria, and the girls would all hang out there, hoping to get Paul to wait on them. But I was the one he'd asked out on a real date, and then another, and another. I realize now that it was because I could do his math homework for him, but back then, I really loved buzzing around town in his sporty candy-apple red convertible. I felt so *cool*. So with-it.

Then Michelle entered the picture. She was barely five feet tall, with curves in all the right places, while I was tall and skinny. And she was from Georgia. Scarlett O'Hara could have taken flirting lessons from her. She would sashay up to Paul, tilt her head coquettishly, and speak in her southern-drawl, kitten-soft voice. The guys practically fell over their own feet trying to get her attention, but she was focused on Paul. It didn't take long for him to forget me.

And then, to make matters worse, she came to my lunch table one day—remember I had a different lunch period from the rest of you that year?—and smiled at me.

"Ya'll wouldn't mind if I sat down with you?"

The other girls at my table stared at her for a moment, then glanced at me sideways since practically the whole school knew Paul had dumped me. I finally found my voice. "Of course not," I said pleasantly, just as if I didn't hate her. Mom had instilled manners in me, after all. I even managed a little smile.

"Thank you. Paul had to stay after math class today, so I didn't have anyone to eat with."

So I guessed she wasn't doing his math homework.

"I found the neatest prom dress this weekend," she said as if we were best friends. "It's got lots of lace and a full skirt, so I'll feel like a real southern belle." She sighed. "Texas is nice, but I do miss Georgia."

Too bad you didn't stay there. I had to bite my tongue not to say those words.

"Who are ya'll going to prom with?"

She addressed the question to all of the girls, but she must have known she'd taken *my* date away. In fact, I think she was asking just to make sure I knew. I really wanted to slap her, but *Texans* held their heads high. Besides, starting a brawl in the cafeteria would horrify my mother.

"Why, Michelle, honey,"—I stressed the word "honey" with a true *Texan* drawl—"No need to worry about me. I already have a date." Surprisingly, the lie came out easily, and it took me a moment to realize what kind of a pickle barrel I had just put myself into.

Michelle stared at me while the other girls at the table clamped their open mouths shut. I wished I had kept mine shut too. Where was I going to find a date on such short notice?

She smiled, although it looked forced. "Really? Whom did you ask? A relative from out of town?"

Politeness could go only so far. How dare she think *I* asked someone? You guys know I don't have much of a temper, but it flared that day. "What makes you think I did the asking?"

She shrugged. "Most of the boys already have dates."

"Maybe most of the junior boys," I retorted, "but a senior asked me."

Her eyebrows went up, as did those of the other girls. "A senior? Who?"

I glanced quickly around and spotted Jim Clayton— senior class president, captain of the football team, with a scholarship to Harvard—sitting at the table behind me. He held himself aloof from the girls who chased after him, probably because he knew he had years of medical school ahead of him, but he probably didn't have a date for prom either. He gave me a puzzled look and I realized I had been staring at him. I turned quickly away. While I couldn't outright lie and say Jim was my date, I might have inclined my head a bit. Everyone at our table turned to look at him and then back at me.

"Jim Clayton?" Michelle asked unbelievingly.

"You'll see," I said.

Thankfully, the bell rang, ending both lunchtime and the horrible conversation. I placed my tray on the rack by the door and left as quickly as I could before I could dig myself any deeper into the hole of my making.

Then, suddenly, there he was. He had followed me out. My face must have been the color of a sunset, but Jim just smiled. "Come on, Amy. Let's go for a walk. We have a few minutes until the next bell."

I looked up at him wonderingly. No doubt he'd heard the conversation. Was he going to lecture me for making something up? Or berate me for involving him? He didn't seem the kind to hurt someone's feelings, but I braced myself anyway. I had been pretty obvious.

He didn't say anything until we got to the little courtyard that students could hang out in after lunch if there was time. It had a few benches, and he gestured to one of them.

I sat down as though the seat was cactus. "I'm sorry," I blurted before he could say anything. "I guess you overheard me back there?"

Jim looked at me intently. "You mean about needing a date for prom?"

My face felt on fire, and I nodded dumbly. "I'm sorry. I...I... Michelle made me so mad because—"

"Because she was goading you," he said and smiled again. "I heard her part of the conversation too."

He had the nicest smile. Not flirty. Just nice. "So you heard Paul broke up with me?"

"We're a small school," he replied. "For what it's worth, Paul never was a team player. He always wants to be the number-one jock on the field."

I stared at him, realizing suddenly that it was true. Paul had to have the fastest car, the most mod clothes, the most attention... I remembered now that he'd showed me every sports article that had his name in it. And he would never talk about the game, just the plays he'd made. I shook my head, wondering why I'd not noticed the self-centeredness before. I guess I'd been too caught up in wanting to be cool...something I definitely wasn't.

"I'm sorry," I said again. "You...you were just the first person I saw, and I... I..."

"I would be glad to be your date."

"What?" I was sure I was hallucinating, even though I'd never touched drugs. "What?"

"I said I would be glad to be your date for prom." He gave me a pensive look. "That is, if you want to go with me."

I probably looked like a gaping fish out of water. I opened my mouth. Closed it. Opened it again. I made a funny croaking sound and then nodded dumbly.

"Good," he said as the bell rang.

"Now I've made you late to class."

He took my hand and squeezed it. "I think being late is worth it."

****

Amy looked at her friends and wiped a tear from her eye. "Michelle did me a big favor, even though I didn't realize it at the time."

"Destiny steers its own course," Jill said gently.

"Can you imagine what life would have been like if I had stuck with Paul?"

Sue curled her lip. "We could always have had Scotty beam him up."

And they all laughed as lasers suddenly splashed across the stage and the crew of the Starship *Enterprise* appeared through the wavering lights.

Chapter Six

"Ladies, are sure you don't mind my tagging along with you each day?" John asked as they docked inside a snug harbor at Key West the next morning.

"You are our historian," Dawn said.

"Not quite. Historians have much more massive knowledge than I do about any given location," he answered, "but since I am going to be writing a series of articles regarding our ports of call, I am doing research each evening so I'll know what to look for the next day. I'd hate to leave out unique points of interest for the magazine's readers."

Sam smiled at him. "Which benefits us too. We have our own personal tour guide."

Smiling back, he bowed elaborately. "At your service, madame."

Sam saw Lynda exchanging glances with Laura, and even Sue was taking an interest in the exchange. To stave off any cutesy remarks, she said briskly, "So where do we start today?"

"Good question," he said as they followed other passengers down the gangplank onto the pier. "For a tiny island that's no more than fifteen square miles, it has a lot to offer."

"Perhaps we should wait until some of the crowd has dispersed before we get started," Jill said. "We do have the entire day."

"True." Sam herded their group to one side of the quay while people rushed past to scramble onto sightseeing trolley buses or head toward the fishing docks to catch charter boats going out.

John nodded. "We can pretty much walk to everywhere from here. While we're waiting, I suppose I could fill you in on the history." He looked at each of them. "Unless that would be too boring?"

"Not at all," Jill said. "I think putting locations into historical context makes exploring more interesting. Half the stuff you told us about Fort Jefferson we wouldn't have known otherwise."

He nodded. "All right, then. I'll keep it short. The Spanish—in particular Ponce de Leon—discovered Key West in the sixteenth century, but Bahamian and Cuban fishermen had been using the island prior to that. Sponges and Cuban cigars were great commodities after a millionaire named Henry Flagler began building an overseas railroad so wealthy Floridians could visit. The fort on the other end of the island was used as a Naval Air Station in both world wars and today serves as a training base. And," he finished, "everyone knows that a number of artists and novelists congregated here after that, as well." He gestured for them to walk. "The island has quite a Bohemian flavor."

Sue laughed. "I think that can pretty much be said for any island in the Caribbean."

"Yeah, it's easy to be laid back with sugary-sand beaches and crystal-clear seas," Dawn said.

"Especially since the trade winds keep the sun from feeling too warm." Cindi sighed. "I could probably spend days and days writing one story after another."

"You wouldn't be the only one. Along with

Hemingway, Tennessee Williams also lived here for a while, as did John Audubon, although he was a painter, not a writer."

"And a myriad of other lesser-known creative souls still find solace here, I suspect," Jill answered as they strolled. "The homes just seem to lend themselves to quaintness and solitude."

"The term I saw on the internet last night was 'Conch Colonial Style,' " John answered. "It's sort of a mix between the simple seagoing lines of New England houses and Spanish lace trim."

"Rather like gingerbread in the southern Colonial style?" Sam asked.

"Precisely. Of course, we'll see lots more of the Spanish lace in the French Quarter in New Orleans, but here…" He stopped to look at one of the houses with its square lines and shuttered windows of a stout northern home with the addition of a second-floor balcony that had curvy wrought-iron railings. "The island was settled by different people over different periods of time, so the architecture reflects that."

"It is interesting," Sam said as they continued on their way. "Huge mansions next to small cottages."

"Obviously, no zoning back then." John quirked his mouth. "Farther along—not on this street, since we're in the tourist area—you'll see some rather dilapidated-looking houses with peeling paint, saggy porches, a few shingles missing."

"I suppose every town has economically disadvantaged people," Jill said, "even here."

"Well…" John inclined his head. "That's quite possibly true, but the ones I was referring to are quite well appointed and kept up inside. At least, from what I read."

Sam wrinkled her brow. "Why would they let the outside look so run down, then?"

He grinned. "Taxes."

The frown deepened. "I don't understand."

"A lot of these homes have been owned by families for generations," John said. "Probably even built by their ancestors. They're not inclined to sell them to outsiders."

"So?" Sue asked. "What difference does that make?"

If he were perturbed by her tartness, he didn't show it. "As you can imagine, property on a small island as unique as Key West is worth millions of dollars. And, like stateside, property is assessed on condition and comparable sales. As long as folks don't want to sell their heritages and the houses don't *look* in prime shape from the street, tax value stays down."

"Hmmm. That makes sense, I suppose," Sam said.

"It seems the inhabitants are pretty savvy," Jill said.

John nodded again. "So were their forebears. In those neighborhoods, the houses are also built really close together. Maybe ten or fifteen feet between—"

"I guess you'd really have to love your neighbor then." Dawn giggled.

"Islanders, like Old West settlers, had to get along. Their survival, at least in earlier days, depended on it," John answered, "but the reason for the closeness was protection from hurricane winds. The closer the homes, the less friction and velocity impacts the buildings."

"I'd never thought of that," Sam said. "Maybe we need to let the cities along the Texas coast in on that secret."

"Too late, I think." Sue shrugged. "We tend not to

learn our lessons from history."

"True. I guess that's why I decided to become a park ranger," Sam replied. "Nature teaches us lots of lessons too."

"Speaking of nature," Amy said, "isn't there a huge aquarium here?"

"There is. Actually, we're very close. Do you want to stop there first?"

Amy looked around at the rest. "Is that okay with you?"

After a chorus of assents, John gestured. "This way, then."

****

Sam had begun to wonder if they were ever going to get Amy out of the aquarium. In addition to alligators, sharks, and poisonous moray eels, there were also turtle exhibits, and Amy had latched onto one of the staff members and a lengthy conversation had involved species, endangerment, and of course the location of the turtle kraals, where giant green sea turtles were kept.

Now, though, they were out on Whitehead Street, strolling past the mix of mansion-like homes and smaller cottages. They stopped at Hemingway's house to look for the famous six-toed cats that might be roaming about, descendants of those that had the run of the property in his lifetime. Unfortunately—or maybe fortunately, depending on how much time Amy would spend if she saw one—none were loose in the front yard.

Their group continued on to the end of the street, which was also the southernmost point of the continental United States. A striped concrete buoy proclaimed it was ninety miles to Cuba and the marker was also surrounded by a throng of tourists.

"I wonder if, on a clear day, you could see all the way across the sea?" Dawn asked. "I was in Norway once and the tour guide said when the weather was good you could see Scotland…or, at least, the Shetland Islands."

"That's probably because you were on a mountain in Norway," Sam said, "and not on an island at sea level."

Jill pointed to a sign. "It's actually eighteen feet above sea level, to be accurate."

Sam almost laughed. Trust a psychologist to be aware of details like that. "I think you get my point anyway."

"Since we're here, would you ladies like for me to take a picture of all of you?" John asked.

"Great!" Jill answered. "That way, one of us won't be missing."

He grinned. "I can come in handy sometimes."

After they'd waited their turn to get a good shot near the buoy, he gestured toward a nearby stand that was selling souvenir conch shells. "This probably sounds a little nerdy, but Sam, would you mind posing by that stand as though you're examining the shells?"

"Me?"

A corner of his mouth lifted. "A little human interest photo to add to my article? You don't dress like a casual tourist, so the pic would add a bit of class."

She could almost hear the thoughts going on inside her friends' heads, and it wasn't about the fact that she tended to wear tailored clothing. "I'm no model."

He tilted his head. "Actually, you are very photogenic. I took a bunch of pictures on the beach in Tulum after we'd walked down the cliff. You were in one of them."

She'd been wearing park ranger cargo shorts that day, with an oxford shirt, but from the way Sue and Lynda were eyeing her, she doubted they were thinking of her sensible clothes. She remembered half her hair had come loose from her ponytail, thanks to the buffeting winds between the cliffs and sea. Did they think… She felt her face warm. "Wouldn't a picture of some pretty young girl buying conchs be better?"

"Not with our clientele. They don't want to look at the typical hollow-cheeked model with no curves. Besides…" He glanced over the rest of their group. "…women of a 'certain age' are trending now. Didn't you hear?"

Sue sniffed. "It's about time men started valuing older women, and the media too."

"I agree," Lynda said. "Men aren't turned out to pasture just because they're in their sixties."

"That's true," Laura added. "Why should it be different with women?"

"Ladies." Jill held up a hand. "I don't think John expected to resurrect Women's Lib by asking Sam to pose for a photo."

"I didn't." He looked somewhat abashed and glanced at Sam. "I, personally, think an older woman has a lot to offer."

Before anyone went off on a tangent on *that* topic, Sam touched John's arm. "I'll pose, okay?"

He grinned like a kid and held up his digital camera. "Fantastic."

She refused to look at her friends as she walked over to the conch kiosk. She just hoped they weren't going to turn this tiny molehill—sea level analogy might be appropriate—into a towering Norse mountain.

****

Sam didn't need to wonder what tonight's theme was because the song that was playing when she walked into the dining room was "Groovin'."

"1967," she said as she joined her friends. "The Summer of Love."

"I think we experienced another summer of love today," Sue said.

Dawn giggled. "You mean *winter*. It's December."

Sue rolled her eyes and Sam almost did the same. Obviously her friends were not about to let this afternoon's episode with posing by the conch shells go, but she could try to dissuade them. "Let's not get started on that."

"On what?" Laura asked innocently, although there was a gleam in her eye.

"Whatever do you mean?" Amy asked as well.

Sam glanced at Amy. It was quite possible that Amy hadn't paid attention to any of the goings on, as interested as she was in going to see the green sea turtles. Still, she did have a dry sense of humor.

"John wanted a photo of someone not dressed as a tourist. That's all. He wasn't insinuating anything else."

Jill raised one eyebrow. "Is this another case of 'the lady doth protest too much, me thinks'?"

"*Hamlet* hardly fits into tonight's theme." Sam sought to change the subject. Unfortunately, the music switched to "Light My Fire" as she spoke, and everyone laughed.

Dawn giggled again. "Perhaps that's a spiritual sign."

"There is nothing 'spiritual' about that song," Lynda

replied. "Have you never listened to the lyrics? Totally physical."

"I know that. I meant maybe the universe was giving Sam a sign."

"Well, I remember 'Age of Aquarius' playing when we got on board," Cindi said.

"Stop being so helpful," Sam said to her and then looked at the others. "We're sounding like we're back in high school."

Jill lifted her brow again. "Isn't that kind of the purpose for this cruise? Our fiftieth reunion and all that?"

"Yes, but…we're talking like we did when we had high school crushes." Sam shook her head. "I doubt John is coming on to me."

Sue snorted. "He didn't ask any of the *rest* of us to pose for a picture."

"For heaven's sake. You are making too much of this. I am not some young bar-fly."

"Well," Laura said, "he did say he liked older women."

Sam wished she had ordered a drink when she came in. "He *said* he thought older women have a lot to offer. He meant—"

"Oh, we're pretty sure we know what he meant," Laura interrupted with a wink. "I don't think it was your opinion on the state of the world, sorry as it is."

"Will you lighten up?" Sam looked around for a waiter. "I could use a drink."

"Here. I haven't touched this." Cindi slid her glass of wine over to Sam and looked at the rest of the group. "We really should stop teasing Sam."

There were a few rumblings, and Jill looked thoughtful. "You know, it would be fine if you wanted a shipboard fling."

Sue nodded. "Why not? You're a grown woman. It's not like you're looking for a happy-ever-after."

"I agree," Dawn said. "Have some fun. If the guy wants to shag you, go for it."

"For sure!" Laura said. "If I weren't married, I might make a pass at the guy myself. He *is* good-looking, you have to admit."

She couldn't argue that point. John did have a very debonair composure, probably because of what he did for a living. It had been years—actually at least a decade—since she'd had any kind of romantic encounter. Something stirred inside her…just the briefest of sensations, like a match held to kindling that hadn't caught yet. Sam pushed the thought away. Now she was being as ridiculous as her friends. Fantasizing about a shipboard romance was about as absurd as believing *Love Boat* endings. Besides, they only had two more nights, the ones in New Orleans, before they'd be docking in Galveston. If the man had wanted to…*shag*, to use Dawn's British slang, he would have made a move before this. She was being silly. "I'm not twenty-something."

Just as she said that, "Let's Spend The Night Together" began to play, and she groaned.

"An omen," Dawn said again. "I really think the universe is sending you a message."

Thankfully, the subject was dropped with the arrival of more wine and, as the music changed to "White Rabbit" so did the conversation.

"Gosh, remember when we thought psychedelic was groovy?" Dawn asked.

"Well, Gainesbury was pretty Hicksville," Sue said.

"The guys were still dancing the Cotton-Eye Joe."

"And that was when country wasn't cool," Laura added with a laugh.

"The guys thought getting beer with a fake I.D. was a big deal too," Jill answered. "No one thought of dropping acid."

"I don't think anyone in town had even tried weed," Lynda said. "We all thought it risqué to smoke a cigarette."

"Hmmm," Sam said. "That all kind of changed when Electra moved to town our sophomore year, didn't it?"

"It sure did," Sue said. "She had actually spent that summer in San Francisco with the hippies."

"And *lived* in Haight-Ashbury!" Amy said. "She even had a black light and some of those posters that glowed in the dark."

"She made it sound so fine to be able to hang loose and do your own thing," Laura said.

"Yeah, it was, like, totally far-out." Dawn mimicked the Sixties' slang. "We all wanted to grow our hair long and wear flowers in it."

"To say nothing of long muu-muu dresses and scruffy sandals," Lynda said. "And I was crazy about anything tie-dye."

"My parents wanted to know why I was wearing a Mercedes-Benz emblem for a necklace." Dawn grinned. "It was really a peace emblem."

"Make peace, not war." Cindi looked around the group. "That was the only thing my parents found at all decent about the whole hippie thing."

"I think that was 'make *love*, not war,' " Sue said.

Cindi shrugged. "I didn't think it wise to correct

them."

They all laughed, and Sam shook her head. "My grandfather had been in World War II and my father and uncles had all served too, so you can imagine how well either of those ideas went over."

Lynda nodded. "My parents freaked when I brought home an album by the Grateful Dead."

Sue looked wistful for a moment. "I think the thing I really envied about Electra was that she'd actually gone to the Monterey Pop Festival and seen some famous performers. She even said she'd met some of them, but I don't know if I believe that."

"I guess it's safe to say we were all pretty impressionable," Sam said. "Even the guys."

"Especially the guys." Dawn laughed. "Don't you remember how all of them wanted to go out with her?"

Sam grimaced. "Probably for all the wrong reasons. There was all that stuff about free love, remember."

"But we girls really didn't think about it as free *sex*," Jill said. "Not at that time. We'd all been too sheltered." She hesitated. "Or, at least, I was. I thought the guys all really liked her because she was so pretty and so…knowledgeable about the world."

Sue rolled her eyes. "She sure was."

Sam gave Jill a thoughtful look. "Did you think your guy was hooked on her too?"

Jill turned pink. "I hate to say this, but I was so jealous of her. There was a week when I didn't see or hear from Wade, and I was sure it was because of her. I thought I was going to die if he broke up with me."

Sam smiled at her. "Sounds like there's a story coming."

"I guess maybe there is." Jill looked around. "Okay,

I guess it's my turn anyway, so let me tell you how stupid I was."

****

Jill's story: 1967

One look at Electra, the day she enrolled at Gainesbury High, was all I needed to start me thinking about keeping an eye on my boyfriend, Wade.

Electra was a senior, as was Wade, and she was beautiful. Not just pretty or cute. Beautiful. Her long auburn hair was streaked from the sun, her strangely colored amber eyes matched the golden color of her skin, and she moved with slow, gliding grace, never appearing ruffled by anything.

Maybe that was because she was stoned most of the time.

Of course, we didn't know about the effects of marijuana at the time since none of us had used it. We just thought she was exotic because she had actually spent the Summer of Love in San Francisco. Flower Power was going to win over blood and violence. To us, the city was a romantic place and all the kids—the Hippies—who'd gone there were wanting to make the world a better place.

And Wade was a rebel. Not that he had a cause any more than James Dean did, but he was always talking about leaving Gainesbury, leaving Texas. Going to the Promised Land…in this case, California. After all, that's where it was happening, right?

The day I saw him in the cafeteria with Electra, hanging on her every word, I knew I had to take drastic action. I rushed over, practically falling over him in my eagerness to grab his arm—just to show Electra whose guy he was—and began jabbering about all the fun we'd had at the lake before school started.

And—I hate to admit this, even now—I didn't stop at that one time. Oh, no. I made an effort to find Wade between classes, before school, after school… I'm surprised I didn't glue myself to him.

Not that it made that much difference. Electra had a way of getting what she wanted. Especially attention from guys. Since she'd spent the summer in a hippie commune where sex was—presumably—free with no commitments, the guys all thought she was easy. But— since I was observing her as closely as a scientist with a dangerous mutant lab experiment—I realized she was also somewhat aloof. She'd be friendly and all touchy-feely, but then she'd back off. Instead of being mad at being led-on, the guys were all intrigued. So was I, but for a different reason. I desperately wanted to know how she managed to do that, so I could work my wiles—ha-ha!—on Wade.

Of course, my maneuvers blew up on me. I still remember that night…

It was a Saturday, and after a local movie, Wade and I went to Herb's Hamburger Haven for a coke and fries. Electra was there, surrounded by boys, so I immediately started talking about how much of the movie I'd missed because we'd been snuggling. Wade gave me a curious look—since we hadn't done all that much snuggling— and when we passed Electra, he stopped.

"Hey, El. How have things been going?"

El? He knew her well enough to call her *El*? The thought made me furious and I didn't even hear her response, although I remember she laughed and so did he. Had she been "getting to know him" behind my back? I must have made some kind of noise, because

Wade glanced at me.

"What's wrong?"

Somehow, I managed to sound calm. "Wrong? Nothing's wrong. Really." Then I couldn't resist adding, "Why?"

"I don't know. You seem kind of off your form tonight." Then he glanced at Electra and back to me. "Look," he started to say, but I interrupted him.

"I think I'd like to go home now."

He looked surprised, but didn't say anything. Instead, he took me straight home, and he didn't mention a date next week, either.

Once inside the house and safely in my room, I cried and cried, afraid I'd really made him mad. Why had I been so touchy? He'd only exchanged a few words with Electra—in a crowded place—and my temper had rocketed. I realized I had to stop being so jealous. I really was going to lose him forever if I kept this up.

Eventually, I stopped sniffling. Wade always called on Sundays. I'd explain tomorrow how silly I'd been.

On Sunday afternoon, the phone rang five times, and each time I sprang up to answer it. Each time it was for my mom or dad or my sister. Well. Sometimes he called in the evenings.

By ten o'clock I knew there would be no call. I debated whether I should call him or not, but my pride took over. Back then, boys were supposed to do the calling.

Monday and Tuesday passed in a tearful state. Because Wade was a senior we didn't have classes together, but I didn't see him in the halls where I usually did. Then I remembered the counselors had made some schedule changes that week because of enrollment numbers. Had his schedule been changed? Why didn't he call to tell me?

The only good thing was I didn't see him with Electra, either.

Wednesday passed, and Thursday. Had Wade dumped me for her? For once, I wished I had been friendlier with her. Maybe I could find something out.

My little sister asked me why I didn't just go over to his place and find out what he was doing. I shook my head. She was only twelve. She didn't understand. Besides, by now anger had taken over. I certainly was not going to chase after him! He owed me an explanation, but I wasn't going to grovel for it.

I ached miserably that Saturday night. Wade and I hadn't missed a Saturday night date in almost six months. Even worse, what if he was out with Electra? It would be all over school on Monday if they'd been seen on a date. I wasn't sure how I was going to cope with that. My mom and dad kept sending me worried looks, but thankfully, they were tactfully quiet.

The phone rang then, but I made no move to answer it. It wouldn't be Wade, and I didn't feel like being social.

"Jill!" Mom called from the kitchen where the phone was. "It's for you."

I stumbled toward the kitchen in no hurry. "Hello," I said dully.

"Jill?"

For a moment, I stood stock still. Wade! It was Wade! My heart hammered so fast I was afraid it might pop out of me.

"Y…yes," I said.

"Sorry I haven't called you, but I've been really

sick. It started with a sore throat and coughing last Sunday, and by Monday, I'd lost my voice."

Relief flooded through me like a broken dam. He hadn't been with Electra! He hadn't been *able* to talk!

"Ah... are you still mad at me?" He sounded uncertain. "I wasn't trying to flirt with Electra or make you jealous."

I started to say I wasn't mad *or* jealous and I didn't care about Electra, but I realized Wade knew me too well. I had been mad *and* I had been jealous. So I decided on the truth.

"I thought you had a thing for Electra."

He started to laugh, only it turned into a cough. When he could speak again, he simply said, "I have a *thing* for you, Jill."

The words thrilled me, but stupidly all I could think to say was, "You do?"

"Yes. I've been miserable this last week thinking you were mad and I wasn't able to do anything." He hesitated again. "I've been meaning to ask you, and this is hardly the best moment, but I want things straight between us. Will you wear my class ring?"

"Will I wear..." I wasn't sure I heard the words right. Then I decided I wasn't going to let the opportunity go. If I hadn't heard right, he'd have to correct me. "I would love to wear your ring and be your steady."

"For real?"

"For real." I grinned like an idiot. "Because I have a thing for you too."

****

Sam smiled at her when she finished. "And you got your happily-ever-after."

Jill nodded. "We've been married forty years and it

83

still seems like yesterday that we tied the knot."

"That's how I feel too," Cindi said.

"And me," Laura said.

"Good for you guys."

Lynda pasted what somewhat resembled a smile on her face, while Sue just looked away. Sam sighed. How would life have turned out if any of her relationships had turned out better? Jack O'Neill had once jokingly said that maybe they should marry so they could continue arguing day *and* night. Not that any of her friends knew that. Of course, he hadn't *meant* it. Who wanted to spend their lives arguing? Although, oddly enough, she'd always felt energized and ready to take on the world after one of their…discussions. And Jack had seemed to feel good too.

Maybe the reason neither of them had married was because they were both weird.

She pushed the thought out of her mind and smiled at Jill again. "I really am glad for you."

And she meant it. She really did.

Chapter Seven

"New Orleans!" Sam breathed in the humid air, warm even though it was December. "I sometimes think this city is more tropical than the Caribbean."

"I love New Orleans," Sue said, "although not for the weather." She looked around as their group stood on the riverwalk. "It's the birthplace of jazz, after all."

"We should be able to get our fill of that," Sam answered, even as she heard distant strains of a trumpet's wail, no doubt a street performer farther down at the French Market. "Anyone for beignets at the most famous café in town, to start the day?"

Cindi laughed. "I think we all had a light breakfast just so we could savor those!"

"I'm sure there's not a single calorie in them," Lynda deadpanned as they headed toward the eatery.

"Zero calories for tourists, anyway," Cindi replied.

"It doesn't matter," Laura said. "We've only got two more days before we head back to Galveston, so we may as well indulge."

Jill nodded. "New Orleans is the perfect place to *indulge*. French cuisine, Creole, Cajun, seafood—"

"Don't forget the hurricanes at that special restaurant!" Amy said. "The first time I had one of those, I practically needed help walking."

"Hmmm. I wonder if their main bar still has those hundreds of beer steins hanging from the ceiling?"

"Or the champagne bottle lamps and the mirrored bar backs?" Laura asked. "I always felt like I was stepping into a private gentlemen's club."

"Which is why I prefer the patio bar," Lynda said. "It feels more like those tiny courtyards tucked away behind homes in the Quarter."

"Yes, more New Orleans atmosphere," Cindi agreed.

"Well, it's a little early to find out this morning, but maybe we can stop by before we return to the ship this afternoon," Sam said.

"Speaking of the ship, I didn't see John waiting for us this morning," Jill said.

Sam shook her head. "He told me he was going out to several plantations today to review them for his magazine."

Dawn gave her a sideways glance. "And *when* did he tell you that?"

"He sent a text last night."

Her eyebrows went up. "A text? So you've exchanged phone numbers?"

Sam wasn't going to let herself be baited. "He asked for my number when we went to Tulum."

"Aha! I knew there was a reason you guys went down that cliff to the beach by yourselves."

"Don't be silly." She hoped the warmth she felt on her cheeks was due to the sultry air. "I'd told him we liked hearing about the historical research he did and we'd like to hear more. He gave me his phone number, so I gave him mine. End of mystery."

Dawn giggled. "I think the real *mystery* is why you haven't shacked up with him yet."

"Will you stop pursuing that line of thought?"

"That probably is a good idea," Jill said. "It's really not our business anyway."

Dawn shrugged. "Just sayin'. *I'd* do it if he were interested in me."

Sue grinned. "Well, New Orleans is known as the Big Easy, so why not?"

Before Sam could comment on that, Cindi intervened, changing the subject.

"You know, I had a weird experience the first time I came here."

"You mean voodoo?" Lynda asked. "There was plenty of that here, too. Marie Leveau, the voodoo queen herself, is supposed to be buried in St Louis Cemetery Number One. Maybe we can visit her later."

"No." Cindi shook her head. "I mean like I'd been here before. In another time."

"Déjà vu?" Sam asked.

"Sort of, I guess. I was still in college. A friend of mine and I had just stepped off the bus on Canal Street and turned onto Bourbon." She drew her brows together as if remembering. "I'd just taken a few steps, and the sounds of traffic stopped. I didn't hear my friend talking, either. Then sound started again, but this time, I heard the clopping of horses' hooves—"

"There are horse-drawn carriage rides available for tourists, you know," Lynda said.

Cindi shook her head, her eyes taking on a faraway look. "Not on Canal or Bourbon. Anyway, the horses were clopping on cobblestone, not pavement. And there were ladies in saloon-type dresses, hanging over the balconies, calling out to men below."

She blinked, refocusing on the group. "And then the scene was gone. All the noise of honking cars and hawking vendors returned. My friend was still talking as though nothing had happened, but I felt like I'd stepped through a moment in time to the 1800s."

"Well, some of those upstairs rooms probably had been brothels," Jill said. "The French had a more relaxed view of such things, and New Orleans catered to the wealthy, even then." She smiled. "Maybe you'd seen a movie not that long before and it triggered your imagination. You are a writer, after all."

Cindi quirked a corner of her mouth. "I write *children's* stories. Besides, I hadn't seen a movie in months. I'd been too busy studying."

"Hmmm. Maybe it's true." Laura looked around the group. "Maybe Cindi did step through some kind of time portal, if only for a minute."

"You mean like in *Outlander*?" Sue swept her glance up and down the street. "New Orleans may have history, but I don't think there are any standing stones around to walk through."

"It wasn't like that," Cindi said. "I was walking on the sidewalk, and suddenly, I wasn't on a sidewalk. I was still there…just…not…just not in this century." She took a deep breath. "It's still as clear as if it happened yesterday."

Sam saw several of their friends giving Cindi skeptical looks. She, herself, had never been one to rule out possibilities just because there was no logical reason to be given. She'd had her own strange sightings and odd sounds, out in the wilds, that were not explainable. She laid her hand on Cindi's shoulder as they entered the café they'd sought.

"If stepping back in time is possible, New Orleans is certainly the place for it."

****

After they'd finished their beignets—and licked the powdered sugar off their fingers—they headed back toward Jackson Square, where the three spires of Cathedral Basilica of Saint Louis, King of France, towered in white wooden majesty over the waterfront.

"Louis the Ninth was the only French king to ever achieve sainthood," Sam said as she tapped the guidebook she'd picked up on ship the night before. "And he was crowned in 1226 at the age of twelve and canonized in 1297."

"What did he do to gain sainthood?" Jill asked.

"Well, he was captured in one of the French crusades and died in Africa as a result, but he was also known to be a very just and fair monarch. He abolished trial by ordeal and introduced the presumption of innocence into the court system." She tapped the booklet again. "Some called him the monk king, even though he was married."

"Compared to some of his descendants, who lived and spent lavishly, he probably was," Jill said. "The French Revolution didn't happen because Louis the Sixteenth was a kind and generous soul."

"True." Sam tucked the booklet into her pocket. "Shall we go inside?"

Their next stop, a half hour later, was the old Ursuline Convent on Chartres Street, a few blocks from the church.

The convent-turned-museum was a stately two-story building with three attic dormers and a portico entry with a balcony above. Unlike the wood cathedral, the convent was done over in white plaster. Inside the entry, a beautiful winding staircase made of cypress wood greeted them.

"This is actually the oldest building in the Mississippi Valley, designed in 1745 and finished in 1753." Sam smiled as she looked up from the guidebook. "The nuns ran it as a school for young girls, too."

"Orphans?" Jill asked.

"No. Well, maybe later. Originally, the girls were brought over from France to marry and populate the area to preserve the French bloodline."

"Ugh. Sounds too much like being sold," Lynda said.

"True, but remember this was the eighteenth century."

"And women were chattel in England even in the nineteenth century," Laura added.

"I'm glad I'm living in the twenty-first, then."

"I think all of us are," Sam said.

"Well, with the exception of Cindi," Dawn said with a grin. "She went back to the nineteenth, remember."

Cindi colored and Sam decided to return to the subject at hand. "The girls were called 'casket'—or 'casquette'—girls because of the small chests they carried their belongings in when they came here."

"It's kind of like the marriage mart in Regency romances, isn't it?" Laura looked thoughtful. "Although I can't imagine how nuns would allow any kind of dances and parties and such."

Lynda grimaced. "If those girls were brought over to be sold off to old men, it wouldn't matter."

"We don't know that they were *old*," Sam countered. "The French just didn't want their blood mixed with the Spanish...or the colonists, for that matter."

"Still."

"There really weren't many options for women back then," Jill said. "Even in the Fifties when we were little kids, women were basically expected to get married and have children."

"Yes, and the only "careers" open to us were nursing or teaching...or being a secretary." Cindi looked around their group. "Of course, most of you defied those odds—park ranger, vet, psychologist"—she gestured to Sue—"and one of us even made it to professional musician."

Sue shrugged. "I was always the one crazy about the music."

"But that doesn't mean teaching isn't still one of the most important careers someone could have," Jill said. "If no one had taught us to read, we'd all be in sorry situations."

"That's true." Sam said. "And, if it weren't for teachers, none of us would have gone to college, either. Besides"—she waved in the direction of what once were classrooms—"the girls did get an education, which a lot of the local population didn't."

Another small group of people joined them then, and they proceeded to tour the museum. The bells at St. Louis Cathedral started tolling and, with the still city air, they sounded like they were coming right from the convent. For a moment, Sam seemed to hear the muffled whisperings and shuffling slippers of dozens of girls as they were called to Hours in the chapel. Then she shook her head. Cindi's story of stepping back in time must had gotten to her.

Or...perhaps New Orleans was as haunted as the legends said.

****

91

The theme that evening was the 1969 Woodstock festival. Not surprising, Sam supposed, as she sat down at their table, given their location. They'd encountered several street musicians that afternoon with top hats turned up on sidewalks for tips. There had even been a brass quartet at Lafayette Square when they'd taken the St. Charles trolley to the Garden District. On their way back, they had heard a pair of trumpeters doing two-part harmony in one of the famous circular areas that dotted the city.

But right now, the sound system on the ship was belting out "Purple Haze."

"Jimi closed the festival, you know," Sue said, closing her eyes to sway to the music. "Of course, it was eight-thirty on a Monday morning when he did."

Sam drew her brows together. "Your older sister attended Woodstock, didn't she?"

"Yes. Jan was attending college at Syracuse, not all that far from Bethel." Sue opened her eyes. "And I always envied her for being there." She sighed. "I tried to catch a bus to join her, but my parents found out and grounded me."

"We'd all just graduated high school. None of our parents would let us go," Sam said. "According to them, it was a bunch of lawless hippies all spaced out on drugs and having orgies."

Sue grimaced. "Our parents thought the Beatles were dangerous thugs, too."

"Didn't your sister get into big-time trouble with your parents when they found out?" Amy asked.

"Yeah, but by the time they got in touch with her, it was all over," Sue replied. "It wasn't like they had cell phones or texting back then."

"Even if they had, being on a farm in rural New York, there'd probably be no signal," Cindi said.

"Not that she would have been able to hear a phone anyway," Laura said. "There were massive speakers blaring that probably punctured a few eardrums, not to mention a half-million kids swarming around."

"But…can you imagine that? Really? *Imagine* it!" Sue closed her eyes again, then opened them. "That massive stage on the hill so everyone could see the performers—"

"*If* you had binoculars," Lynda said. "People were spread out over two hundred acres."

Sue waved her hand dismissively. "So? Everyone moved around since they were there for three days."

"Three hot, muggy and muddy days."

"I doubt it was paradise," Amy said. "I remember the news saying there weren't enough toilets or medical facilities—or even enough food and water, since the event planners weren't expecting the massive crowds."

Sue frowned at her. "But that's the beauty of it. It was three days of *peace* and music. The farmer, Mr. Yasgur, who rented them the land, brought food, and pretty soon other locals were doing it, too. And everyone *shared*."

Sam nodded. "What's truly surprising is the lack of violence. Very few fights. Very few arrests. Can you think of what a crowd that size would do today if they were stuck for three days in the middle of nowhere?"

"I shudder to think," Laura said, "especially with as much civil unrest as there is these days."

"Not that there wasn't unrest in the Sixties," Jill said, "what with the Civil Rights movement and the anti-war protests."

"A lot of the kids who went to Woodstock were probably the same ones that hung out at Haight-Ashbury," Amy said, "and they were a lot more mellow. The drugs they were using weren't Fentanyl or meth."

Lynda grimaced. "And if they were tripping, they probably didn't even know they were there."

"You guys are all missing the point," Sue said. "It was the *music*. Santana. Credence Clearwater Revival. Blood, Sweat and Tears. Melanie. Crosby, Stills, Nash and Young...when Young was still with them." She looked around the table. "Most of those bands were just starting out. They weren't well known yet. Imagine being some of the first to hear those groups play live! Just *imagine*."

Dawn stifled a giggle. "Now you're beginning to sound like John Lennon."

Sue lifted on shoulder. "The lyrics of that song actually sum up the Woodstock experience quite well, I think."

"Well," Sam said, "Woodstock may not have been my first choice of concerts to attend, but I can see why Sue would have wanted to go." She looked at the others. "It was Sue's idea for us to form a band in the first place, and she was the one who held us together when we weren't so sure."

"That's true," Lynda admitted. "None of us would have actually been on a stage if it hadn't been for you, Sue."

"I can remember how excited you were when we got our first real breakthrough," Amy said.

"Getting that offer was probably the most important moment of my life," Sue replied.

"So..." Sam smiled at her. "Relive it for us."

****

Sue's story: 1968

I remember how disappointing—for me—our first participation in a Battle of Bands was. I was so excited we'd gotten a spot to perform in the Houston competition. Important people from recording studios and talent agents were going to be on hand, and I foolishly thought we'd be sure to get signed on by one of them. All that stage mascara was smeared by my tears. Luckily, we had been the last to perform, so no other bands were in the backstage area.

Yet…Dawn saw the whole thing completely differently. She practically flew into the dressing room, waving her drumsticks.

"I think we did it," she said. "We finally broke through!"

When I reminded her we hadn't gotten any offers, she shook her head and said maybe we didn't get signed, but a couple of scouts had been watching us. They were tuned in, she said, and then she sat down on the floor and started practicing a drum roll.

Even I had to smile at that. Of course, I quickly sobered when I remembered that to actually get on any charts we first had to be signed. I started analyzing our group. We called ourselves the Cicadas—which were insects with a high, shrill sound—but it seemed the In thing to do since there was so much play on words with the Beatles being "beetles." Was the name lacking something, though? Would a change help? I knew we weren't as good as we could be, and we weren't well-known, other than in some of the small towns around Gainesbury.

There were also kids who didn't like an all-girls pop

group, either. The Supremes, Ronettes, Shirelles, and Martha and the Vandellas were all Black groups with a unique sound. We were trying to do rock. But why should only guy bands—the Stones, the Animals, Steppenwolf, and the Beach Boys—be successful? It was the *music*—the *rhythm*, the *beat*, the *lyrics*—that mattered.

I know each of you wanted to be a part of it. We started fighting for it right after our freshman year. We argued with our parents over organizing. We begged to audition for any teen dance that was going to happen. We tolerated the guys—and even the girls—being skeptical. And we worked hard to buy our instruments and take lessons.

We even learned about sound systems, although I have to admit Drake Colton had been a big help with that. I even fancied myself in love with him for a while. I thought we could go places—New York, California— and do big tours. He even said he'd be our manager, and I was ecstatic. None of us was really good with money— we could barely keep our sheet music in order—so we were pretty much in the hole most of the time. Drake said he'd take care of it and we'd soon be *making* money. Of course, all that changed when I wouldn't let him go all the way with me.

Then I got depressed. Maybe our band would never work. Maybe we were all getting tired of it and that was why our sound wasn't tops. We all realized being in a band wasn't glamorous—it was a lot of hard, long hours of practice. Sometimes we'd have to drive fifty or sixty miles to play at some small town event, and a lot of those seemed to be on Sunday evenings, which meant we were all tired for school on Monday.

Then there were the girl things...all of us sharing mirrors and slathering on make-up and hoping it didn't ruin our complexions when the greasepaint started to run as we sweated behind footlights.

Yet none of *you* complained, and I wondered if I was letting you down.

And then, after a gig at the County Fair shortly after that Battle of the Bands, I watched all of you afterward. Your faces were flushed, your eyes glowed, you were full of excitement, and one of you made the comment— I forget who—that there was something to being "on stage" in front of an audience and you loved the thrill of applause. And I remembered the reason I wanted to perform.

It was *fun*. If we didn't get signed, so what? The music made me feel alive.

Life does tend to be ironic, though. It was only a few nights after that, as we were testing amps, tuning strings, and checking the lights on the stage of our school auditorium for our Fall Festival performance, when Mr.Wilhelm, our principal, came over. He had an odd look on his face, and he was holding a letter.

"The school received a letter today from the event organizer at the Houston Battle of the Bands. It seems one of the agents that attended was interested in the Cicadas."

I have to say he looked a little bewildered, but he did manage to smile as he handed us the letter. Then, of course, he dropped the bombshell.

"Actually, the agency sent two scouts to listen to you tonight. They're out front right now."

Oh, my God. I think we all practically did a collective swoon. This was our chance! If we got signed, there'd be bigger events…promotions, billing, publicity. We would be on our way!

Half an hour later, the auditorium was full. We all had resisted the amateur urge to peek through the curtains to see where the agents were seated. If we wanted to be signed, to become *professionals*, we had to act the part.

Thankfully, if unexpectedly, the students started to stamp their feet, whistle, and call out for our band. I wondered why they were doing that, but I was only grateful they did. It would make us look wildly popular.

I remember asking if everyone was ready, and we each took a deep breath. We straightened our Beatle-like pantsuits, swung our hair back behind our shoulders, and smiled as the curtain rose.

I strummed a chord, the rest of you kicked in, and we were on. The Cicadas were on.

****

"It was fun, our senior year," Sam said, "even if we didn't become rock stars."

"But we did get signed by that agency," Amy said. "That was really an accomplishment in itself."

"It probably wouldn't have happened if the kids hadn't been acting like they did before the show," Jill said. "I remember one of the agents saying they liked the enthusiasm."

"You can thank Jack O'Neill for that," Laura said. "He somehow found out about the agents out there and he spread the word around to make sure those guys would know we were popular." She smiled at Sam. "He probably did it for you more than the rest of us."

Dawn laughed. "He'd tease Sam to death—or at least until she was ready to hit him with something, and then he'd turn around and do something nice. Maybe you should have hung on to him after all."

Sam shook her head. "We went our separate ways after graduation. Probably saved us both our sanity."

"It *is* too bad he isn't on this trip," Jill said. "Who knows what might have happened if you'd seen him again."

Sam shook her head again. "I think this cruise has gotten to you guys. You've all gotten overly romantic. First John—"

"Whom you haven't pursued, in spite of our pokes," Dawn said.

Sam ignored that. "And now Jack, who isn't even here to defend himself."

Sue raised a brow. "He probably wouldn't need *defending*."

"He isn't *here*."

"Too bad," Jill said. "We won't know if he's changed or if he still has that little mischievous boy inside him like he did at our graduation."

"No, we won't," Sam answered.

But maybe it would have been interesting to find out.

Chapter Eight

"How was your day at the plantations?" Sam asked John as he joined their group on the wharf the next morning.

"Well, the atmosphere will definitely appeal to our readers who have a romantic bent," he said as they started walking toward the French Quarter. "It's hard not to appreciate the beauty of long driveways overhung with weeping willows and leading up to columned veranda-encircled mansions. Not to mention perfectly manicured lawns with magnolia trees and bougainvillea in every hue of pink and red. Easy to imagine sipping a mint julep on the porch on a hot afternoon."

"Reminiscent of Tara and Twelve Oaks?" Cindi asked.

"In a way. The ballrooms are still there, and a lot of work has been done to preserve the architecture, along with period furniture pieces. Original crystal, china, and silver from the 1800s are encased in the hutches of some of the dining rooms, although I doubt they are actually used for guests these days."

"It must have been hard—and expensive—to import fine china and silverware back then," Jill said.

"I'm sure it was, especially if the French citizenry had to pay British tariffs on imports," John answered, "but there was also a black market operating for luxury goods."

"Isn't there always?" Lynda grimaced. "Only these days, it's drug cartels."

John smiled. "Well, opium was legal back then, so drugs weren't particularly in demand, although French brandy was a popular commodity for those who operated in the gray world."

"And where did they get their products?" Dawn asked. "France isn't exactly close."

"Piracy, right? Pirates roamed all over the Caribbean, so it would have been easy—relatively—to intercept ships passing through." Laura looked at the group. "We learned about that at Fort Jefferson, remember?"

Sam frowned. "Yes, but wasn't the age of piracy over by the 1800s?"

"You're right," John answered. "One of my favorite topics of research has been the 'Golden Age of Piracy' but Blackbeard, Calico Jack, Anne Bonne, and the rest of them were gone by then. Piracy was, after all, a hanging offense. The lure of capturing fortunes remained, though. So those who sought to overtake ships on the high seas went a more legitimate route and obtained a Letter of Marque—basically a legal document that said a pirate was working for a country that was at war with another and so had the right to capture the enemy's ships."

"Sounds like something a lawyer would cook up," Lynda said.

John laughed. "Well, the city attorney of New Orleans in 1814 was a friend of its last pirate, but he didn't come up with the idea of the letters."

"The last pirate?" Dawn asked.

"Jean LaFitte. Actually, he called himself a

privateer. He had a Letter of Marque from Cartagena, as Columbia was fighting for independence from Spain. It was less expensive—and less complicated—to hire privateers than use the military. The government's goal was to destroy enemy ships, but privateers were allowed to keep the bounty, so it benefited both."

"I guess the bounty was lucrative enough that pirates—privateers—felt it worth the risk?" Sam asked.

"Yes. In addition to gold being sent back to Spain from Mexico, there were also imports of luxury goods like spices, brandy, linens, silks, furniture, utensils, and tools being delivered to the Spanish aristocrats. Cargo like that would have been fair game for Jean, since he had his letter."

"And he sold those goods to the French in New Orleans?" Jill asked.

John nodded. "And at discount prices, since he didn't 'declare' the goods to the tax man."

"Then he couldn't very well just put them up for sale in the marketplace, could he?"

"He didn't have to. He set up his headquarters in Barataria and used his blacksmith shop in New Orleans as a front for his private entrepreneurial pursuits."

"Which were smuggled goods," Lynda said.

"Depends on how you want to look at it. If you could get high quality goods relatively inexpensively, why would you pay the added tab of tariffs and taxes? Remember, the French didn't care for interference from the new US government." John smiled. "It didn't take long for businessmen to realize they could make a better profit by dealing with Jean and still keep their prices less than the tax-enhanced amount. Lafitte also held special auctions on occasion—generally for unique items—on

Cheniere. The French aristocracy went wild for those. And, to add a little mystique as well, he referred to the place as 'The Temple.' "

"I suspect that was a play on words?" Sam asked. "Like in the 'temple of vice'?"

John laughed. "Lafitte was known to have a sense of witty humor."

Lynda raised a brow. "A pirate with a sense of humor?"

"He was an educated man who spoke four languages."

"Regardless, his 'temple' was still in Barataria, which is swamp land. Wasn't it dangerous for folks to venture out there?" Jill asked. "From what I've read, that area is similar to the Everglades...a jungle of low-hanging moss on cypress, tall marsh grass, murky water, quicksand...and little sun to penetrate the shadows—"

"To say nothing of alligators, snakes, rodents, and disease-bearing mosquitoes," Amy added.

"That too," Jill said. "I would think it would be really easy to get lost and never come out of the swamps."

"True," John replied. "but Jean and his men knew the swamps and bayous well and the government men didn't, so it made a perfect hideaway."

"Kind of like that Everglades song by the Kingston Trio, right?" Cindi said.

"Precisely, but, to answer your question, Jill, his men would ferry their elite customers out privately in canoe-like pirogues." John smiled again. "And he would wine and dine them, too."

"In the swamps?"

"The terrain made it difficult for anyone who wasn't

invited to approach, much like medieval moats around castles," John answered, "but that didn't mean Jean and his men lived like refugees. Quite the opposite. He'd acquired a lot of Spanish gold from his conquests. From all accounts—and by now, I'm sure you've all figured out I have done quite a bit of research on Jean Lafitte—he was suave, sophisticated, and charmingly charismatic, which appealed to both ladies and gentlemen. He definitely enjoyed the finer things in life, including use of some of that china, crystal, and silver that was confiscated."

"Not exactly the picture of a pirate as we would imagine," Jill said.

"Privateer," John corrected. "And that interest in culture might well be the difference between them."

"We passed a place yesterday on the corner of Bourbon and Bienville that was named after him," Sam said, "but we didn't go in. Was that his blacksmith shop?"

"No, the smithy is farther down. That would have been the Absinthe House," John replied. "These days, it's a saloon serving absinthe cocktails, but a little over two hundred years ago, General Andrew Jackson met with Lafitte there to enlist his help in fighting the British."

"The Battle of New Orleans," Cindi said. "I remember Johnny Horton sang a song about it."

"You do have an odd way to remember history," Lynda said.

She shrugged. "It's a teaching tool and actually works with children."

"Well." Sam thought it best to divert that conversation before it became an argument. "I guess the

United States didn't think Jean was a pirate then."

"Actually, it did. Or, more correctly, Governor Claiborne did." John grinned. "That's where the city attorney comes in. Jean was tired of having a price on his head, so he contacted John Grymes—the attorney—and offered him ten thousand dollars to work as his emissary to convince President Madison of his full loyalty to the States. He'd never attacked an American ship and he wanted get Claiborne off his back." His grin widened. "It worked. And in New Orleans—the French never having taken to the governor, who was a straight-laced Virginian—laughed for months."

"So the President pardoned him?" Cindi asked.

"Actually, not until after the Battle of New Orleans. 'Old Hickory' had arrived with only eighteen hundred soldiers, who were battle-weary from quelling an uprising of Native Americans on Mobile Bay. They were also out of ammunition and needed more weapons. Jean—ever the entrepreneur—had kegs of gunpowder and a stash of weapons taken from ships he'd raided. He also had his own one-thousand-strong personal army. And…well, you know how that battle turned out."

"Yes, I remember in that song they defeated the British despite running out of ammunition. Something about grabbing an alligator…" Cindi stopped and frowned when Lynda rolled her eyes. "Song lyrics *do* make it easy to remember history."

"I remember Johnny Horton wrote several other history-related songs, like *North to Alaska,*" Jill said. "He must have enjoyed history as much as you do."

"And speaking of history…" Sam interjected, turning the conversation back to the subject at hand, "didn't Jean Lafitte eventually move to Galveston?"

"Yes, but not until three years later, in 1817. Unfortunately, even though Jean was a free man, Governor Claiborne never gave up. He confiscated the goods at the warehouse on Grand Terre and auctioned off Jean's ships, claiming that all of that property was ill-gotten gains of a pirate. Rumors spread that LaFitte was still practicing his illicit trade and New Orleans' aristocracy began to turn their backs on him."

"Just like London's *haute ton* in Regency romance," Dawn said.

"Snobs," Lynda said, "and ingrates. If Jean—whether pirate or privateer—hadn't helped Jackson, we might all be singing *God Save the Queen.*"

"That's true. Thank goodness for Jean Lafitte." Cindi looked at John. "Can you fill us in on the rest of the history? It'll be interesting to know about the Texas part, since we'll be back in Galveston tomorrow."

"I'd be glad to, but I think I've lectured long enough for today." He stopped for a moment and pulled some papers out of his coat pocket and handed them to Cindi. "You might want to read these."

"What are they?"

"Notes I took last night on the Galveston experience."

"We don't get into port until late afternoon," Sam said. "You'll have plenty of time to tell us all about Texas tomorrow."

"Well…" He paused. "I actually will not be continuing the trip. I'll be leaving the ship this afternoon."

"Oh." She didn't quite know what else to say. "Are you needing to fly back to New York to meet a deadline?" Even as she said it, it sounded rather asinine.

The ship had free internet service, and he'd obviously had his computer along. When he hesitated, she felt a prickly feeling run down her spine, something that had happened a few times before and was always an ominous warning of impending peril. "Never mind—"

"I'll be spending a few more days here." He didn't look directly at her as he spoke. "My wife will be joining me for a long weekend."

Absolute silence followed that remark, and Sam wished she could step through Cindi's time portal to another world.

****

Her friends gave her covert looks when she joined them for dinner that evening. Not that she blamed them. She'd probably moved like a zombie for most of the afternoon.

After the stunned silence following John's announcement, her group had all started chattering like a bunch of squirrels as if he'd done nothing more than mention the weather. She'd pasted a smile on her face—and kept it there until her cheeks actually hurt. She was the one who insisted that he stay with their group for the rest of the day, even though he'd made an offer to excuse himself. She wasn't about to let him—and especially her friends—know the effect those words had on her.

Not after actually entertaining the idea of having a shipboard fling. The group had been urging her on all week, reminding her that John sought her out every day and always complimented her, which he didn't do with the rest of them. He just needed a little encouragement from her, they said, because of the times we live in. With the Me Too movement and women stepping forward with accusations of improper intentions, no man was

107

going to be brave enough—or stupid enough—to make an advance on his own.

That had all made sense, and it had been a long time since she'd indulged herself. She was an adult and not a blushing maiden who thought it would go anywhere, which made the last night on board a safe time to approach the subject. She thought John would agree.

And, since he had conveniently forgotten to mention he had a wife—he didn't wear a ring and there was no telltale tan line on his finger—he might well have agreed if she'd brought the subject up before today. Sam grimaced. She didn't get involved with married men. Ever.

"Are you okay?" Jill finally asked.

"Yeah. I'm fine." Sam took a deep breath, grateful she hadn't shared her thought with her friends and they'd never know how close she'd come to succumbing. "Didn't I tell all of you he wasn't interested in me?"

They all glanced at each other, but apparently had made a pact not to badger her, because they let the remark pass. Jill nodded slowly.

"Well, then. I propose we have a toast to the Sixties, since this is our final night on board." She signaled their waiter, who hovered just out of hearing distance. "I see you have a bottle ready…is it something special?"

He gave a slight bow, which didn't make the tray he held waver one bit, and then turned the bottle for their inspection. "Not wine tonight, madam, since the theme for this evening is Whisky A-Go-Go. California law at the time forbade a bar from using a specific alcohol in its name, so the owners of that historic establishment borrowed the Scots spelling." He smiled. "And since they did, we are serving drams of single malt tonight, compliments of the captain."

Sam noticed for the first time the small shot glasses placed in front of each setting and she smiled—genuinely—for the first time that day. Straight whiskey sounded just fine.

"I wonder if they actually served this at the Whisky A-Go-Go?" Dawn asked as they finished their drams. "It's good."

"I don't think scotch was a real popular drink on Sunset Strip in the Sixties," Cindi said. "Remember that was a young crowd, more likely to prefer cheap wine or beer."

"Besides, the big draw was the go-go dancers," Amy said.

Sam looked to the stage, which tonight featured a neon-lit stand-up bar. Above it were suspended two gilded cages in which two of the ship's female crew were dancing to the theme song of "Secret Agent Man." "I remember the short fringed skirts and white boots."

"And look at those cages," Laura said. "I can't believe they actually had girls dance in cages suspended above the bar."

"Which meant the guys spent more time looking up than they did at what they were drinking," Lynda said. "What a sexist image that was."

"Best to put it in context." Jill shrugged. "Women's Lib hadn't happened yet."

"And the DJ played records from a suspended cage," Sue said, "although I suppose he didn't draw the same attention."

"Anyway, I thought those white boots were cute," Dawn said. "Remember when I wore a pair to school and got sent to the principal's office because the dress code said boys couldn't wear boots to school? A couple of them got mad and said a girl shouldn't be able to wear boots either."

Lynda snorted. "So the *guys* wanted equal rights then."

Amy glanced at Dawn. "Didn't Jack defend you, though? Actually told the principal it was just a fashion statement like Beatle haircuts?"

"That argument didn't go over particularly well with Mr. Wilhelm, since mop tops weren't allowed either," Sam said.

"I imagine it didn't, since Jack wore one," Amy said.

"He almost got suspended for that too." Sam shook her head. "Somehow he managed to convince Mr. Wilhelm that it wasn't really a Beatle cut. It was just long."

Laura laughed. "Jack always was good at getting out of things."

"That particular time, what saved him was that his hair didn't actually touch his collar so he—as he put it later—wasn't breaking dress code." Sam grinned. "Of course, that was because it was a pep rally day and he was wearing a school T-shirt that didn't *have* a collar."

Jill smiled. "Which I'm sure he didn't point out to the principal."

"Probably not."

"He certainly managed to get by with a lot," Laura said. "Remember when he brought the rattlesnake to school?"

Sam grimaced. "At least it was dead."

"But poor old Mrs. Bennett nearly fainted when she saw it sticking out of his jacket, She couldn't even finish the English lesson." Amy frowned. "I don't recall how he got out of that one."

"He told the principal that Mr. Trenton, the biology teacher, wanted us to dissect a snake," Sam shook her head again. "And the truth was…that he *had* mentioned that in class."

"So Jack didn't get suspended that time either," Cindi said. "He seemed to have the luck of the Irish."

"Well, his last name *is* O'Neill, after all," Amy said.

"I don't think being Irish had anything to do with it," Sam answered. "Jack knew his parents would ground him if he got into real trouble."

"*Real* trouble?" Lynda raised her brows. "He *stayed* in real trouble."

"Not really. Pardon the pun." Sam lifted a shoulder. "I grew up next door to him, remember. I think he liked pushing the boundaries, but he never did anything actually bad."

"Not even mean, either." Cindi looked at Dawn. "How many guys would defend a girl wearing go-go boots?"

"And to Mr. Wilhelm, no less," Laura said. "He wasn't exactly a fan of rock-and-roll."

"You can say that again." Lynda rolled her eyes. "He thought the second British invasion was worse than the first."

"And yet bands like the Beatles, Dave Clark Five, and Herman's Hermits all wore suits, for pete's sake," Dawn said.

Sue laughed. "Unlike Woodstock. But some performers had raunchy moments, like being drunk on stage, or dropping acid and falling off the stage…" She sobered. "You know, all those musicians from that time period really *felt* the music. In *here*." She touched her heart. "I think that's why some of them are still around today."

Sam nodded. "I think our generation felt strongly about everything. The Hippie movement. Equality. Civil Rights. Vietnam—"

"It was a real shame, though, that the returning Vietnam vets didn't get treated with the respect we give veterans now," Jill said.

"True," Sam said. "Especially since almost all of them were drafted and didn't have a choice about serving."

"They didn't even have to be returning," Cindi said. "Some of them felt the hostility before they were even sent overseas, yet they knew they had to do a job."

Sam drew her brows together. "Didn't that become a big thing between you and Pete?"

She nodded. "I almost lost him before he saw combat."

Jill looked around the group and then at Cindi. "So tell us about it."

****

Cindi's story: 1969

Senior year, for me, was magical. Pete's family had moved here that summer, and I first saw him at the swimming pool one afternoon. I thought he was a real hunk, all golden tan and blond hair, lean with enough muscle to look strong, but not too much... Anyway, it didn't take long before we were "accidently" splashing each other, and I was thrilled when he asked me out.

And I know I was lucky. We didn't argue about anything. Saturdays were date nights. Sundays we alternated going to each other's houses for dinner after church. I watched him play football on Friday nights, and he was my escort to Homecoming. For Christmas he gave me a silver bracelet, and in the spring we went to Prom. I was happy. He was happy. At least, I thought he was. No. I *know* he was. Then.

But two weeks after graduation, the letter came. His draft number had been called and he was going into the Army.

My first reaction was disbelief. Nobody got drafted *immediately* after high school. But Pete was nineteen and he hadn't applied to college. He said he didn't really know what he wanted to do…maybe work and save some money first.

My next reaction was to be mad. Angry. Furious. The Army was going to take Pete away. No. No. No! Why now? Wasn't President Nixon talking about withdrawing troops from Vietnam? They didn't need to take him… Maybe he'd flunk his physical? Even as upset as I was, I knew that wouldn't happen. He wouldn't fake a problem, either. He was too honorable. That was one of the things I loved about him. But there had to be something we could do to keep him home!

Of course, there wasn't. He was being sent to Fort Benning, Georgia. It might as well have been halfway across the world. I remember trying really hard not to cry as I watched him walk onto the plane—we could do that back then, remember?—I even managed a quivery smile because he said he didn't want to see tears or he wouldn't let me come to the airport. "Don't cry," he said. "I'll be coming back."

But as soon as he disappeared, I broke down. A ticket agent even came over to see if I was all right. How could I explain the misery I felt seeping into every bone of my body? Pete was leaving. He would be going off to fight. Through my tears, I could see the plane taxi away from the gate.

"Cindi."

A voice came through the mist that seemed to surround me. A voice I dimly heard through the fog in my mind. I turned, wiping my tears, not caring that I rubbed my mascara-stained fingers on my new skirt. Nothing mattered.

"Cindi." Pete's mother's voice was gentle. "Come along to the car now, dear." She put an arm around me. "He'll be back before we know it. Just a few weeks."

I let myself be led away, but I remember hating planes and hating the war.

Pete did write me faithfully, telling me about boot camp…the drills, the firefighting training, the rifle-range practices, the strict regulations, the importance of not questioning his superiors. That had to be the hardest for him.

Horrible loneliness set in. After I read his letters I would sit alone in my room, clutching the latest one to my heart. I lost weight. My mom got worried about me, but all I felt was a dull, aching throb. His being gone was awful. I saw him at every corner when I walked outside. I watched for his old yellow car and listened for the sound of the familiar knock in the motor when it idled. Once I actually did see it, but it was his younger brother driving.

The one thing I did force myself to do was to keep up with the Cicadas. You guys probably saved me from a nervous breakdown.

Then, suddenly, the nine weeks were up. Pete, distinguished-looking and strangely different in his uniform, was home!

We spent his fourteen-day leave trying to cram in everything. Afternoons, we walked, or sat and talked. Evenings, we went to the movies or the drive-in. We went to the lake and someone threw a party. I felt like my old self again. Happy. Content. My mother was so glad I was smiling and laughing again. It was like Pete had never been gone.

The leave was up too soon, but parting this time didn't seem as bad as the first time. Pete was being stationed at Fort Hood, and it wouldn't be that long before he could come home on a short leave.

I tried not to fall into a funk again. College would be starting soon for me, and my mother kept reminding me I had that to look forward to. Still, my thoughts were centered on Pete. I relived the memories of those two weeks over and over. The letters came only once or twice a week now. I knew he was busy, but I still wished I could look forward to one each day. I cherished the ones that he did write, even if they were filled with everyday occurrences at the base. It made me feel close to him.

College was strange. The first terrifying thing was the size of the campus. Ten thousand students! That was nearly four times the whole size of Gainesbury! All the new faces—strangers. "Profs" not "teachers." The long assignments that made term papers in high school look like short essays. The tests were hard. I had to be attentive and cram or I'd flunk out. The college didn't care, and I was beginning not to.

I'd always been an honors student and involved in extracurricular activities, even before we formed our band. I'd always had so much energy and enthusiasm. I knew I was slipping, but then I got big red Fs on two assignments that I thought had been easy.

Pete would be so disappointed if he found out—I had to pull myself up.

Looking around that classroom, I realized I didn't know a single student. Hadn't bothered to introduce myself or start any conversations. I didn't even know what latest songs were hits or who the new groups were. I'd lost touch with all of you.

Slowly I made the effort to get out of my melancholy. I joined a couple of clubs, made friends with the girls on my floor in the dorm. I stopped writing sad poetry and made my letters to Pete sound more upbeat.

His next leave was just after the holidays. Evidently, the Army thought it would make its new soldiers too soft if they were allowed to go home for Christmas. I'd missed going to the Christmas Eve church service with him and exchanging presents the next day. I sent him a wool muffler that I knitted myself, even though he could only wear it when he was out of uniform. He'd had his mother buy me a sweater.

Pete was quiet when he came home. He had changed. He didn't want to talk about the Army, which I could understand, but I couldn't seem to get through to him. It was as though there was some invisible wall between us. He'd smile when he caught me watching him, but his face, in repose, was hard, the set of his jaw stubborn. I wondered if that was what the Army did to a boy. Then I reversed that thinking. Pete had become a man.

His last night home, he told me he'd gotten orders. His next duty was Vietnam.

I remember my head reeling. I thought I might faint. This shouldn't be happening. He was supposed to stay here in Texas. Safe.

But I think I'd known, ever since he got his draft notice, that this would be the outcome. There were still too many troops over there. But what if he got killed? I knew I'd die too. And I also knew I could not let him know that.

"I can't ask you to wait, this time," he told me. "I may not be back. Or I might be wounded or injured and end up in a wheelchair the rest of my life. Or I might not be right in my mind. I don't want to have to kill anyone, but I may be forced to."

"Stop!" I said, but he went on anyway, saying the words I never thought I'd hear.

"We're through. I want you to forget me."

"What?" I was sure I hadn't heard right. "You know I will never forget you."

"You must."

"No. I will be waiting for you when you come home. In whatever condition."

He stared at me for a moment and then turned and left without saying another word. My head was spinning as I watched him drive away. Somehow I managed to get back into my house and to my room. He couldn't have meant what he said. We loved each other. Time would make him understand.

But time went by. The letters stopped coming. I didn't know if he'd stopped writing or if letters weren't being sent back to the States. Still, I wrote him every day. I didn't know if he'd get them, but I hoped he'd sense I was with him in spirit.

And I knew I would wait.

Forever.

****

Their group was quiet after Cindi finished. Sam looked around at each of them and took a deep breath. There really wasn't anything else to say.

Chapter Nine

"I thought *The Buccaneer* was a really appropriate movie last night, even if it wasn't actually filmed in the Sixties," Cindi said as their group assembled on the lido deck for a buffet breakfast. "We got to see a visual interpretation of the Battle of New Orleans."

Dawn nodded. "Just like John told us about yesterday."

Sam kept her face impassive and hoped her color hadn't risen. Now that she'd had a night to sleep on it, she was doubly glad she hadn't made a fool of herself with him, and it was a relief to know he was off the ship. They wouldn't be putting into port at Galveston until four o'clock this afternoon, which meant they were trapped on board all day. She'd have hated to run into him.

"I'm not sure I would have cast Yul Brynner as Jean LaFitte," she said to change the subject. "All the pictures we've seen show Jean with long, dark hair."

"The producers did put a little hair on him," Cindi said.

Laura shook her head. "Not enough, though, but I did think Charlton Heston as Andrew Jackson was a good choice."

Sue laughed. "A little more muscular and probably better-looking than the real Jackson."

"I think that's what Hollywood does," Sam said

rather dryly.

"Well, I'd like to see a movie about him and his crew while they were in Texas," Cindi said. "The notes that Jo—I mean, the notes I looked over last night were really interesting."

Bless Cindi for being sensitive. Sam just hoped it wasn't because her own emotions were showing on her face. Jill was also casting a wary glance at her, and she didn't want to be psychoanalyzed at the moment. "Since the ship is launching a pirate-themed lunch for our last afternoon, why don't you give us the scoop on them in Galveston?"

Cindi pulled out the notes from her bag before anyone could protest a history lesson. "First of all, he named his new base Campeche."

"Is that Spanish?"

"Actually, it is derived from a Mayan term—too bad we didn't know about this when we were in Tulum—'ah kin pech' which means 'place of snakes and ticks.' "

"Probably appropriate for the island, especially then," Lynda said.

"I doubt Jean was referencing the Mayan," Cindi replied. "More than likely he was thinking the location was similar since it was part of the Yucatan at the time and he'd been there."

"Wasn't Texas under Spanish rule when he landed?" Jill asked.

"Actually Mexican, which itself was under Spanish rule, but it was fighting for independence. That made it lucrative for the pirates—er, privateers—to work out of Galveston."

"That makes sense," Jill said. "Jean had been raiding the Spanish under a Letter of Marque from Cartagena, so

I suppose he could do the same with Mexico."

Cindi nodded. "That would eliminate him being labeled a pirate."

"So did he set up the same kind of business he'd had in New Orleans?" Dawn asked.

"Pretty much," Cindi answered. "The notes say he built a big house at the east end of Galveston, painted it red, and called it Maison Rouge." She glanced at the papers. "But it was really half fortress, with cannon barrels protruding from portholes in the upper story."

Lynda gave her a droll look. "That would be a welcoming sight."

Cindi grinned. "Well, his guests wouldn't see them, since the cannons faced out over the Gulf."

"Defending his territory from other pirates, I guess?" Amy asked.

Cindi shook her head. "Not so much pirates as Governor Claiborne. The man was determined to see Jean LaFitte—and his men—hang."

"Some people just don't know when to give up," Jill said.

"And he was one of them. Three years later he managed to convince President Madison to send the *U.S.S. Enterprise*—not the Star Trek one!—to Galveston. The envoy—a Lieutenant Kearney—ordered Jean to leave the area because he was stirring up too much trouble and the United States didn't want to agitate Spain."

"So did he leave?"

"Not just then. He stalled. But Lieutenant Kearney returned the following year—this time with a war fleet behind him—and with harsher orders. Either Jean left or he and his men would be blown to smithereens."

"Not a good alternative," Lynda said.

"No." Cindi looked at the notes again. "But the interesting part is that the next morning, when the naval fleet was positioning themselves to attack, Jean and his men were gone. There wasn't a trace of them or their ships. He'd disappeared overnight. And…he'd burned Campeche to the ground. All that was left was smoke."

"So where did he go?" Dawn asked.

"Well, that is the mystery of it," Cindi said. "To this day, no one knows."

****

Sam looked at the stage as they entered the dining room for the farewell lunch. The theatre director had gone all out. There was a replica of the foredeck and bowsprit of a Spanish galleon, complete with a water barrel strapped to the forward mast. Due to ceiling limits, it was only about eight feet high, but it gave the illusion of extending upward. Several of the crew were dressed as swashbucklers and were engaged in swordplay on deck.

"Impressive," Laura looked over the stage slowly. "I think I like this set the best of all of them."

Sam nodded. "It looks like they saved the best for last."

"And it's different," Jill said. "We've had Sixties-based themes all week."

"A pirate theme is fitting, though, given that Jean Lafitte operated in both New Orleans and Galveston," Dawn said. "And, he was probably the last of the famous pirates—"

"Privateers," Cindi corrected.

"Whatever. It's still fitting since this is our last lunch on board, too."

The antics on stage continued as they ate their lunch, which consisted of a spicy shrimp Creole with French baguettes and crème brûlée for dessert. Just as they were finishing, there was a shout from one of the actors on the stage.

"Stowaway! We've got a stowaway!"

Several of the "pirates" gathered on the foredeck, where the lid of the water barrel had been pried open and a man was being helped out. He was bearded, and a bandana covered his head. He wore only a vest, showing muscular, tanned arms, and tight, ragged shorts that showed off equally muscular legs.

Dawn grinned. "Kind of like a male version of the girl stepping out of a bachelor party cake."

"I didn't know we had any Chippendale-type guys on board," Sue said.

"Well, he may not be a Chippendale, but he'll do," Dawn looked at Sam. "I guess you were right. They did save the best for last."

"I…" Sam frowned. There was something familiar about the stowaway. She watched as the pirates wrestled with him on stage, one of them pulling his bandana off. She gasped suddenly. There was no mistaking that burnished gold hair.

The stowaway was Jack O'Neill.

****

"Were you surprised?" Jack asked half an hour later when they'd finally managed to get a table for two in the piano bar.

"That isn't quite the word to describe it." Sam took a sip of wine while she collected her thoughts. "How did you end up on that stage? No. Wait. I'm sure that's a story in itself." She put the wine glass down, since she

123

probably needed a clear head for his explanation. "How did you end up on board the ship in the first place? You weren't on the class list."

"That's because I knew I wouldn't make it to Galveston before the ship left. Like I told everyone earlier, I was single-handling my sailboat across the Gulf. Unfortunately, no amount of wind or engine is going to make a sailboat go faster than her hull speed."

"Yes, I got that part. But how did you get on board *this* ship?"

"Well, I put my boat in dry dock—it needs an overhaul—and was planning on surprising you when you disembarked in Galveston. When I checked in with the cruise office to find out what time you were getting into port, the nice lady at the desk said you were spending two nights in New Orleans and then heading back. That got me to thinking. So I asked the nice lady if, by any chance, I were to fly to New Orleans, would it be possible to sail the last day back with you."

She refrained from rolling her eyes. No doubt there had been a good amount of flirtation involved with the "nice lady." She said, "I thought the ship was at full capacity."

He grinned. "I got lucky. They'd had a cancellation."

John. John had gotten off a day early because of his wife. Sam's mouth twitched. How ironic.

"What's so funny?"

"Ah…nothing. Really." She didn't want to go into *that* story. "It was nice of you to come and surprise all of us, though."

He sobered. "You, Sam. I wanted to surprise *you*."

She drew her brows together. "Me?"

"Yeah. When I got the invitation for the reunion, it started me thinking. We had a really good relationship in high school."

She raised a brow. "You teased me constantly."

"I liked arguing with you."

She lifted her brow higher. "So you wanted to see me so we could get into an argument fifty years later?"

Jack shook his head. "No. Well, maybe…but not seriously."

"I'm not sure I understand."

"Of course you don't. How could you?"

He ran a hand through his hair and, in that instant, Sam was transported back in time and they were both eighteen again. How many times had she seen him do that? It had always been an endearing characteristic to her. "Umm…you aren't making sense, exactly."

"I know." He took a deep breath. "Like I said, I got to thinking. I've had my share of…relationships, over the years. There were even a couple of times I almost got married, but something always seemed…not quite right." He shrugged. "Part of it might have been being gone for months at a time. No room on board an oil tanker for a woman…even if I were the captain."

Sam nodded. "I can relate. I spent a lot of time in remote places too. Not exactly conducive to being a wife or raising kids."

'Exactly. I've spent the last five years on board my sailboat, cruising the South Pacific. I love being out on the water with nothing but the horizon ahead, but…" He shrugged again. "It's a solitary life. I'm not sure I want that anymore."

"You're going to sell your boat?"

"I don't think I'll ever do that, but maybe some

Caribbean island-hopping?" He gave her a sideways glance. "Maybe I could use a first mate?"

Sam blinked. "You're asking me to go cruising with you?"

"Maybe." He ran his hand through his hair once more. "Nothing to decide on right now, since it'll take a few months to get the boat refurbished. But...you live here in Houston, right?"

"Kemah, actually."

He brightened. "I've rented an apartment there, since it's close to the boatyard. Maybe...we could take some time to get reacquainted and see where it goes?"

See where it goes. She'd almost done that with John. But Jack wasn't John. She'd known Jack fifty years ago. She suspected, given his latest escapade of jumping out of a water barrel, that he hadn't changed all that much.

She tilted her head as a man joined the female pianist on the bench—much like a heroic actor did at the Oscars one year—and they began "Shallow."

She'd always thought she was happy...but perhaps it was time she looked for a new horizon. They certainly weren't getting any younger. Sam smiled and raised her glass. "You're on."

He clicked his glass to hers. "To the future, then."

Epilogue

Three months later, on March 11, 2020, a day before the world shut down due to COVID, Jack and Sam set sail.

Like Jean LaFitte, they left with their destination unknown.

Afterword

If you enjoyed reading about the real Jean LaFitte, both American hero *and* anti-hero, you might also enjoy three historical romances in which he plays a part.

The Last Pirates is a single-author anthology by Cynthia Breeding. Please turn the page for an excerpt from each of the three novellas in that anthology.

The Last Pirates: The Bayou Prince
by
Cynthia Breeding

Christian Picard kept an eye on his target, Fiona Gordon, standing by a potted palm next to the French doors that opened onto the veranda of the governor's ballroom. Even if she had not had hair the color of a pumpkin, she would have been hard to miss in this crowd of young Southern belles swirling in their white and pink tulle dresses to the fashionably new quadrille. The young woman was nearly a head taller than the other girls and somewhat gangly, as though she hadn't quite become accustomed to her height. Her dress, a somewhat drab gold—or maybe it just looked drab next to the flaming color of her hair—had a high collar and fitted waist, unlike the smooth lines and low décolletage worn by the debutante society of New Orleans. Not that Fiona's modest dress hid the fullness of her breasts, he noted with interest.

"Are you going to gawk at her all night or make a move?" his friend Andre Dubois asked with a grin.

"What do you suggest I do? I cannot simply walk over to her and introduce myself as one of Jean Lafitte's privateers, can I? We have all been declared outlaws…and her aunt and chaperone is Mrs. Claiborne, to boot."

Andre's grin widened. "Jean was tempted to attend

129

this ball himself, just to see the governor's wife again…even if she only knows him as 'Mr. Clement.' "

"Unfortunately, Governor Claiborne knows Jean only too well," Marc Rochelle, Christian's other friend, said with a chuckle.

"With Pierre Lafitte rotting in jail, Jean couldn't take the chance of joining him," Christian said, "even though he chafed about not being able to outwit Claiborne again."

"That's why we—or specifically you—are here. That girl is not only staying with her aunt, right here in the governor's mansion, but her father is Captain William Gordon, serving under Commodore Patterson. Patterson is no friend of Jean's either. We need to keep tabs on him," Andre said. "The girl can be a gold mine of information for us."

"Not to mention, with the British burning Washington D.C. last week, Jean needs to know where the English navy is, as well," Marc added. "Barataria is defensible; hell, even Patterson can't navigate the bayous and swamps, but British ships patrolling the Gulf waters would interrupt our…er, *trading* business."

Christian looked over to Fiona again. She had not moved, nor made any attempt to smile at the one or two still-wet-behind-the ears swains who had headed her way, only to veer off. Did she not have a dance card? His eyes roved down her figure. She had nicely flared hips, perfect for providing a soft, comfortable cushion for a man if she were on her back with… He forced his mind off that subject. He already felt like a louse for having to concoct a cover story and gain her trust, only to use her for deceptive means. But there was a war on. The British were rapidly winning, and New Orleans was divided between the aristocratic French and Spanish families and the Americans—a population the Creoles didn't think much better than the British.

Ah. Yes, there was the dance card dangling from her wrist. He wondered why Mrs. Claiborne had not bullied the young men into signing it. Surely, being the niece of the governor's wife had some advantage. Just as he was thinking that, a young man did approach Fiona, taking her card and pointing to his name. Christian watched as she shook her head and turned incredibly red—the curse of anyone with such fair skin as she had. The young man bowed stiffly and stalked off. She had refused to dance? That was unheard of in society. He saw the color drain from her face, and she turned quickly to hurry out onto the veranda.

"There's your chance, man. She's all alone." Marc slapped him on the back. "She may not be the most attractive woman in the room, but she's no crone, either."

"Think of it as duty to your country," Andre added with a big grin. "There are worse assignments than stealing a kiss or two to enthrall a fair maiden."

Christian shook his head and left his two friends chortling about Fiona and a dark veranda. From the little he had observed of her, he did not think she was easily *enthralled*. She had the look of a woman who knew her own mind.

And his challenge was to change it.

The Last Pirates: Treasure of Campeche
by
Cynthia Breeding

Ilsa Drescher's neck ached and she lifted her blonde mane to rub the stiffness out. She'd been sitting in a cramped position, half-buried in a sand dune, peering carefully through blades of Pampas grass, for more than two hours. Far past the foam-crested rollers, a schooner lay at anchor, riding the increasing swells of the Gulf of Mexico. She bore no name nor flag, but Ilsa didn't need to see the Jolly Roger to know it was a pirate ship. Spanish galleons carrying gold from Mexico made the high seas a lucrative business, especially in an isolated place like south Texas.

The men who dinghied to the sandbar to explore the shipwreck that had carried her parents and other ill-fated German settlers wore no uniforms, their bare upper torsos bronze in the sunlight that also caught the glint of gold ear-loops. If Ilsa's parents had survived, she would be in for a sound scolding for even looking at half-naked men, but her parents were gone, swept out to sea by last week's storm that grounded the ship.

One man in particular caught her eye. He was taller than most, and his long, sun-bleached hair blew back from a chiseled face with high cheekbones and a strong jaw. Fascinated, Ilsa watched as his broad shoulders strained and biceps bulged, hauling on one of the ropes attached to the top gunwale of the listing caravel. The other men grunted in rhythm as they heaved on the lines.

"It's no use," one of them grumbled. "We'll never right her."

"We're trying to stabilize her," the tall man answered in a rich baritone tinged with a French accent. "I'll not risk the lives of my men slipping under an unsteady wreck." Even as he spoke, the ship seemed to shudder and then settled more heavily onto her port side. The hole in the hull gaped black in the low tide.

"There." With a nod, he flicked the rope from the gunwale and waded thigh deep into the water. His body sluiced through a breaker with dolphin grace as he made the first dive.

Ilsa held her breath for what seemed an eternity before he resurfaced with a small wooden trunk. She gasped, recognizing it as her mother's.

"Nothin' but clothes," one of the pirates complained as he watched his leader rummage through the trunk.

"Not quite." The captain removed a smaller case which he opened and held up a locket. "This is good quality. Perhaps there's more."

His men needed no further encouragement. Eagerly, each of them dove beneath the waves. Ilsa clenched her fists. That necklace was her father's gift to her mother! She had a good mind to march out there and snatch it from the pirate's clasp.

Before she could move, however, someone grabbed her from behind and pulled her up from her burrow. A large hand clamped over her mouth and stifled her scream. She looked up into the savage face of a giant Carancahua scout. *Mein Gott*! The Spanish monks who'd given her and the few other survivors refuge had warned her of wandering off. Why hadn't she listened?

The pirate's head whipped around at the muffled sound. Surprise registered on his face as she was dragged from the sand, clawing at the man. Heading their way, he called out something in a language that made her captor pause.

Ilsa ceased her struggling to stare at him. He was unarmed and hadn't called to his men to assist him. He must be mad to approach a savage like this!

He spoke to the native again in the same language, gestured toward her, and held up the necklace. The man grunted and held out one hand. The pirate shook his head, smiling, and indicated that Ilsa be released first.

She suddenly found herself sprawled at the pirate's feet. Without taking his eyes from the Indian, he bent slightly and wrapped an arm around her waist, lifting her to her feet as easily as though she were a sack of feathers. For a moment she was pressed against his side and heat seared through her.

"Walk—slowly—toward the dinghies," he said as he released her.

Ilsa hesitated, her eyes on her mother's locket. "That's my—"

"*Now.*"

She could tell he was a man who was used to instant obedience, yet she still lingered as the native fumbled with the clasp to open the pendant. It was the only thing she had left that had been her mother's…

The pirate's eyes turned dark and stormy. "Would you prefer to have us both killed, *Mademoiselle*?"

The clasp popped open and the Caranahua stared at the miniature inside the locket and then he looked at Ilsa and back to the trinket. Horrified, he hissed something at her and threw the locket down, a long knife appearing suddenly in his other hand as he took a menacing step forward.

"Could you use some assistance, *frère*?" a voice behind them inquired mildly.

"I could, Andre," the pirate answered, keeping his eye on the Indian and not turning around. "Is Louis with you?"

"Right here," another man answered as he handed him his sword. "Shall we make quick work of this? There's plundering to be done, and the boatswain warns the glass is falling."

The pirate gave a quick glance at the clouds darkening the horizon. The Carancahua pointed at the clouds and made a gesture toward Ilsa. He muttered something low, then turned and walked away.

Ilsa bent and scooped up the necklace, only to find the pirate's warm, strong hand covering hers.

"Let me see that."

A tingle coursed up her arm and to the pit of her stomach at his touch. How strange. She'd never felt the like. Reluctantly, she released her prize.

He studied the picture inside. "Is this you?"

Ilsa shook her head. "My mother. We look alike. She…she died in the wreck."

His gaze penetrated her, his eyes a clear, rich hazel now that the anger had ebbed. "I'm sorry. Did your father survive?"

Holding back tears, Ilsa shook her head. "Only a handful did. There's a small mission not far inland. The monks have given us refuge for a few days before we head north." She took a deep breath and held out her hand. "If you'll give me that, I had better get back."

A corner of his mouth lifted in a half-smile as he tucked the necklace into a pocket of his wet breeches. "Since you don't do well at following orders, *Mademoiselle*, I'll keep it until we're safely back on my ship."

She tried not to dwell on how those wet pants clung to him and outlined his muscular thighs. The very few men—boys, really—that her overly protective father had allowed to court her hadn't looked like this. She had the strangest urge to want to feel the muscles of his broad chest and shoulders. The priest would surely have her doing penance if he knew! She swallowed, her throat suddenly dry. "Once you're on board and I'm on shore, how will you return it?"

"Because," he said as the quirk became a full-fledged grin, "you're coming with us."

"I most certainly am not! I may have lost my parents. I'm not about to lose my virtue too." Her mother—equally protective—had been quite firm that a girl should be a virgin when she married.

He raised a dark eyebrow. "I'll take care of your virtue."

She felt her cheeks warm. "I'm sure you will." She was two-and-twenty years old; she'd heard stories of what pirates did to women. One of her mother's fears, once they'd reached the warm Caribbean waters, was being boarded by pirates.

"Women are bad luck on board," Louis interrupted. "Let her go."

"I'm afraid I can't do that," he answered. "That Indian thinks she is a devil-spirit because of her picture. He'll be back with others of his tribe to kill her. The monks wouldn't stand a chance in defense." He turned to her. "You wouldn't want to be responsible for a massacre, would you, *Mademoiselle*?"

With a sinking feeling, she knew he was right. The missionaries had only begun to gain the trust of the Carancahua. She straightened her shoulders and looked into his eyes. "My name is Ilsa Drescher. If I am to be your...guest... I will be protected?"

His eyes glinted with amusement. "*Certainement.* You have my word."

She raised her chin. "You're a pirate!"

He grinned again, his white teeth flashing in his tanned face as he bowed low. "Privateer. Marc Rochelle, captain for Jean Lafitte, at your service."

The Last Pirates: A Pirate of Her Own
by
Cynthia Breeding

Having forgotten her parasol once again, Emily Clayton sat on a bench under the merciful shade of a magnolia tree and watched as a majestic schooner slowly glided through the quiet waters of Charleston Harbor toward the wharf. She swatted at a mosquito and lifted her coppery hair from her damp neck. Although it was not yet noon, the day was already hot. Little waves of humidity danced in the air, causing the ship to shimmer slightly as though it might not be real. Indeed, with its dark hull and tanbark sails, it could sail stealthily at night, unnoticed, like pirate ships of old.

She smiled a little to herself. Mama—rest her soul— had always said Emily was over-fanciful. The golden age of piracy had passed, nearly a century gone since then, but she wondered how it must have been to sail the high seas, free to seek adventure in new and exciting places...even to relieve the Spanish galleons of their stolen gold from Mexico. Anne Bonny had done it. A pirate had swept her off her feet, stolen her from her husband, and sailed for Cuba. She became a pirate herself, skilled with both pistol and rapier. How Emily envied the woman's freedom and courage. Of course, she was eventually captured and her father ransomed her, brought her back to Charleston, and forced her into a sedate marriage to some landowner, but at least Anne had the thrill of venturing beyond the confines of prim-and-proper society.

A large, dark cloud obscured the sun, bringing deep shadows to the stately mansions lining the Battery behind her. The air hung heavy and still as Emily turned her gaze away from the ship to the park across the way. Its old oaks were laden with tendrils of dripping moss, but as a slight zephyr of a breeze stirred, she saw not the moss move, but the bodies of Stede Bonnet's twenty-nine pirates swinging from those trees for four days nearly a hundred years ago. She could almost smell the stench of rotting corpses over the briny scent of the sea.

Stede Bonnet had been known as a gentleman pirate, an educated, wealthy French plantation owner in Barbados. The story always reminded her of the rumors of the infamous Jean LaFitte, who had disappeared over a year ago along with his ships and treasure. Before Papa was killed in the war, he'd fought alongside Captain LaFitte in New Orleans and been proud to do so. How she wished she could have met the pirate!

The sun peeked back out, erasing the faint images of long-dead pirates, and Emily gave her body a little shake. She would not allow herself to become morbid. She should be grateful Mama's second husband had given her a home these past two years and even a Season, although she suspected, since she was already eight-and-ten, he was hoping one of the young swains at the various balls and soirees would offer for her hand and relieve him of his responsibility. Unfortunately, none of the young men interested her. They were too conventional, too proper, too willing to accept society's many rules of decorum.

She looked again at the ship. It flew no flag. Where had it come from and what was its cargo? As she watched, two men emerged from the aft cabin and made their way down the gangplank. One appeared to be middle-aged, with slightly graying, dark hair. The other nearly took her breath away.

His hair glistened blue-black in the sunlight and curled against the scandalously open collar of a white shirt that stretched across broad shoulders. The sleeves were rolled up, baring strong and tanned forearms. How totally improper. How totally intriguing. The soft doeskin breeches he wore were almost indecent, hugging well-muscled thighs that rippled as he walked. Emily could just imagine the ladies at one of the many social Societies choking over their lemonades, swooning in shock over such a display of pure maleness. Her breath hitched again, wondering what it would be like to dance the waltz with *him*.

She gave herself another shake. Her thoughts really were running wild today. Such a man would never be received by the matrons of Charleston's elite.

"There you be, child! I should have knowed you'd be by the water." A rather plump, middle-aged black woman huffed her way toward Emily. "Your step-pa ain't none too happy that you were gone this morning."

Emily sighed. Aunty Maisie had been her mother's servant, more friend than slave, and had taken it upon herself to keep Emily under her wing after Mama had taken the yellow fever. Or at least she tried.

"I'm sorry, Aunty. I just couldn't take another morning of calling on those pretentious old biddies, leaving little cards on silver trays, hoping they were receiving."

The other woman frowned. "It's the way of things, iffen you want to catch a rich husband."

Emily turned her head toward the dock, but the dark-haired stranger had disappeared. "What if I don't want to catch a rich husband?"

Maisie snorted. "'Course you do. Your mama would want you to have the best."

Emily blinked back tears. Her soft-spoken mother had always seemed so happy with her Army husband, even if it meant traveling to different posts. Sometimes she thought her mother had married Mr. Jamison simply so Emily would have a place to call home...a house in Charleston and a plantation to retreat to during the summer months.

"I'd rather be happy than rich."

"Ain't no rule you can't be both, child. Now come along, before the master tans my hide for not keepin' a better eye on you."

Emily stood reluctantly. Mama had never allowed any of the slaves to be flogged, but her stepfather had a temper. As a magistrate, he also favored Mayor Hamilton's militant approach to controlling slaves.

"All right. Tell Mr. Jamison I shall return shortly and attend the Library Society's luncheon at two o'clock." At least, a few of those women actually read books and could carry on a conversation.

"He said I was to bring you myself."

Emily smiled. "You know you don't like to get anywhere near a horse, Maisie, and I brought my mare." She motioned over to a rail down the street where several horses stood, patiently swishing their tails at flies.

The slave's eyes widened to show white all round. "Lordy. You rode here by yourself and not in a carriage?

And no escort? Not fittin' and not proper. Lordy, lordy. I be in trouble now, Missy."

"It was a nice morning, and the carriage is so stuffy," Emily replied. "I will explain to Mr. Jamison that I slipped out while you thought I was in my bath." Which was true anyway. "It's only a few blocks, so run along. I'll catch up to you before we reach the house."

Maisie looked as though she were about to argue and then sighed. "You come straight home? No ride in the park first?"

Emily smiled. "I promise." She watched as the servant left, shaking her head and muttering to herself. Walking down the street, she unhitched her horse and led it to a mounting block. She had ridden at various Army posts and even by herself on the plantation; surely, riding a few blocks in the city in broad daylight should pose no problem. She reined her horse around. She wouldn't ride in the park, since she'd promised not to, but it wouldn't hurt to ride along the wharf to Queen Street and then back on Church before heading home.

Emily had just passed one of the three churches the street was named for when she looked up at the Planters Hotel. It had a reputation for goings-on that weren't entirely proper. For women… She blinked. A woman dressed in a man's shirt and trousers stood by the window at the end of the second floor. She certainly didn't *look* a strumpet. Not that Emily knew exactly what a lady of ill-repute would look like. But this one had short hair and no painted lips or kohl around her eyes. The woman watched her, a thoughtful expression on her face.

Was she scrutinizing Emily? Did she disapprove of a woman riding alone on the streets? Emily lifted her chin and continued to ride, turning down Chalmers Street.

Southern society just had too many rules.

A word about the author...

Cynthia Breeding lives on the Gulf Coast of Texas with a very non-spoiled poodle-mix and enjoys walking and horseback-riding on the beach, as well as sailing.

www.cynthiabreeding.com

Thank you for purchasing
this publication of The Wild Rose Press, Inc.

For questions or more information
contact us at
info@thewildrosepress.com.

The Wild Rose Press, Inc.